To Jenna ♡

from Uncle Gerald

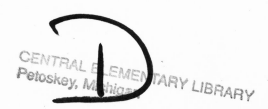

DINOSAURS IN YOUR BACKYARD

Kentrosaurus, a stegosaur, was about 16.5 feet (5 m) long
and weighed perhaps 1.5 tons.
Stegosaurs, plant-eaters all, became extinct
well before the end of the dinosaur age.
They were apparently replaced by the ankylosaurs.

One of the earliest true dinosaurs was *Thecodontosaurus,*
a 10-foot (3 m) forerunner of the great sauropods.

DINOSAURS
in Your Backyard

WRITTEN AND ILLUSTRATED BY

William Mannetti

ATHENEUM   New York

Library of Congress Cataloging in Publication Data

Mannetti, William.
Dinosaurs in your back yard.

1. Dinosaurs—Juvenile literature. I. Title.
QE862.D5M353   567.9′1   81-7998
ISBN 0-689-30906-6   AACR2

Atheneum
Macmillan Publishing Company
866 Third Avenue, New York, NY 10022
Collier Macmillan Canada, Inc.

Composition by Dix Typesetting, Syracuse, N.Y.
Printed and bound by Fairfield Graphics,
Fairfield, Pennsylvania

Designed by Mary Ahern

First Edition

3 5 7 9 11 13 15 17 19 20 18 16 14 12 10 8 6 4

Deinonychus was a small but fearsome predator.
Ten feet (3 m) long and weighing perhaps 150 pounds (68 kg),
it was able to tear apart its victims with
the especially large claw on each of its hind feet.
Such a claw was a characteristic of all dromaeosaurs.

Contents

New Ideas

If you wonder what dinosaurs were like, simply take a good look at birds. For birds actually are a kind of dinosaur here with us today. Now, for most of us this is a startling notion, and not everyone can easily accept it. But in the last several years various scientists have put together information that shows us how birds are descended from dinosaurs, and why we have good reason to believe that birds are indeed a line of dinosaurs. And this is only one of many new and surprising ideas that scientists have formed. Today many scientists tell us that dinosaurs were "warm-blooded," that some were very fast runners, and that many were smart animals. We are also told why dinosaurs became so huge, why most became extinct, and why some did not.

These new ideas about dinosaurs are completely different from the old ones, which portrayed the dinosaurs as slow, stupid, "cold-blooded" reptiles. So we have a brand-new picture of the dinosaur. Like anything else that's new, it has caused us to ask many questions. In the pages that follow, we shall take the new information about dinosaurs and use it to answer as many questions, both old ones and new ones, as we can. We shall also discuss why dinosaurs are among the most important animals to have ever lived; and you will see why you have dinosaurs in your backyard.

DINOSAURS IN YOUR BACKYARD

Stegosaurus was the largest of the stegosaurs, measuring 20 to 30 feet (6–9 m) in length and weighing almost 2 tons.

What Is a Dinosaur?

Answering this question is not easy. In the first place, the word "dinosaur" has no scientific meaning. It is a nonscientific term we use for animals that are placed into either of two groups, or *orders*. The orders have been created by *taxonomists*. (Taxonomy is the science of classifying life forms.) One order is named *Ornithischia*; the other is named *Saurischia*. (The main difference between the two orders is in the structure of the animals' pelvic bones.) Every single animal that most of us have usually just called "dinosaur" can be found in either one order or the other. So, scientifically speaking, some dinosaurs are ornithischians, while others are saurischians.

Of course, explaining that a dinosaur actually is

3

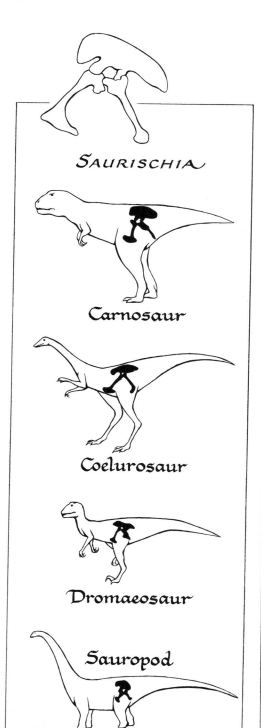

SAURISCHIA

Carnosaur

Coelurosaur

Dromaeosaur

Sauropod

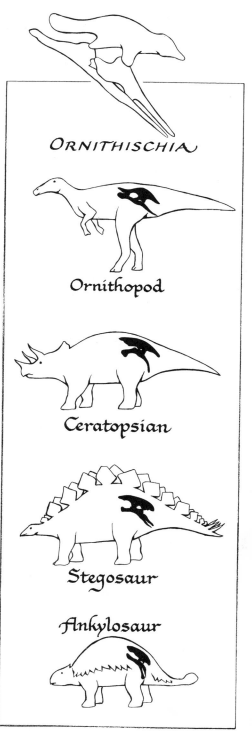

ORNITHISCHIA

Ornithopod

Ceratopsian

Stegosaur

Ankylosaur

either an ornithischian or a saurischian is not really telling us what it is. But doing so does begin to show us how taxonomists look upon dinosaurs. Now, taxonomists can develop a pretty complicated set of names for an animal. They may use over a dozen of them for a single creature. The names result from separate categories that have been created. (A typical list may include the categories: phylum, subphylum, class, subclass, order, suborder, family, subfamily, genus, subgenus, species, and subspecies.) Each one tells us something about the animal we are describing.

Over a century ago, taxonomists placed all dinosaurs (ornithischians and saurischians) into the class named *Reptilia*. They continue to do so today. Thus, taxonomists look upon dinosaurs as having been "cold-blooded" animals, probably covered with scales.

Taxonomists place all dinosaurs into either of two orders. One order is *Saurischia,* which means "lizard-hipped." (Scientists of the 1800s believed that the pelvis of this order was lizardlike.) The other order is *Ornithischia,* which means "bird-hipped." The *Saurischia* order is made up of two groups: the sauropods, and the theropods. The theropod group is further divided into carnosaurs, coelurosaurs, and dromaeosaurs.

The *Ornithischia* order includes four groups: stegosaurs, ankylosaurs, ceratopsians, and ornithopods. The ornithopod group is further divided into iguanodonts, hadrosaurs, and pachycephalosaurs.

Recently, however, some scientists have said that doing this, calling dinosaurs reptiles, is wrong. They say we have made a serious mistake in trying to determine what a dinosaur is. These scientists believe that the dinosaurs of the past *could not have been reptiles*, and they list six reasons why. Each reason is important, so we must take a careful look at each one.

Dinosaurs Versus Reptiles

Over two hundred years ago the fossilized jawbones of a large extinct marine lizard were found in Holland. Because this was the first find of its kind, scientific interest in it was widespread, and in very little time the scientists of Europe correctly identified the bones as belonging to a lizardlike reptile. It was not until the year 1828, however, that the reptile was given the name *Mosasaurus*.

The discovery of *Mosasaurus* was important, for it influenced scientific thought: It caused scientists to accept the idea that huge lizardlike reptiles had inhabited our earth in prehistory. Therefore, when the first bits of *dinosaur* fossils were carefully collected (in the early 1820s) scientists were already inclined to believe that they were looking at the fossilized remains of reptiles. With this belief in mind, they quickly found "proof" of it: The skulls of dinosaurs, the scientists pointed out, were reptilelike, containing the number of openings in them equal to that of modern reptile skulls. Furthermore, dinosaur teeth were very much like those of reptiles. Dinosaurs, then, in the minds of the scientists, surely were reptiles.

Interestingly, there was evidence available at the time that should have caused doubts in the scientists' minds. It was clear that the hip, backbone, and limb structures of the newly discovered dinosaurs were not reptilian at all. One perceptive man, an anatomy professor named Richard Owen, did realize this, but he did not break away from the accepted idea that dinosaurs were reptiles. Instead, in the year 1841, he suggested that the gigantic animals were extraordinary reptiles worthy of a special name. He offered one—Dinosauria—which he had created from two Greek words, deinos, meaning "terrible," and saurus, meaning "lizard." So the word "dinosaur" was invented precisely because there was a visible difference between the fossilized skeletons and the skeletons of reptiles.

Professor Owen's word "dinosaur" became part of our vocabulary. More importantly, however, the notion that "terrible lizards" roamed our earth in the distant past became accepted as scientific fact.

Today, however, this "fact" is not accepted by all. While many scientists continue to think of the great dinosaurs as reptiles simply because their skulls were reptilelike, there are some scientists who say dinosaurs of the past were not reptiles. These scientists came up with this conclusion in one simple way: They carefully examined dinosaur skeletons and then compared what they saw to what they knew about reptiles such as lizards and crocodiles. They found that dinosaurs differed from these reptiles in six important ways. Each difference, they say, is a reason for believing dinosaurs could not have been reptiles. Here are those differences:

(1) The fossilized skeletons of dinosaurs show that their legs inserted *under* their bodies. This is not the case with reptiles. If a reptile has legs (not all do: snakes, for example, do not) they are always inserted into the *sides* of the body. The upper parts of the legs (above the knees) are horizontal, or sideways. This forces the reptile to crawl when it moves about. Lizards, crocodiles, turtles and tuataras all have this reptilian crawl. It is a crawl that is immediately noticeable when compared to the walk of a mammal. A mammal

The Komodo Dragon has its legs inserted into the sides of its body. This is a reptilian characteristic. The young lion pictured here shows that its legs insert *under* its body. This is a mammalian characteristic. Notice that the top section of each of the lion's limbs (from the elbow to the shoulder, and from the knee to the hip) is straight up and down. This is not the case with the Komodo Dragon or any other reptile: The top sections of reptile limbs are horizontal, or sideways.

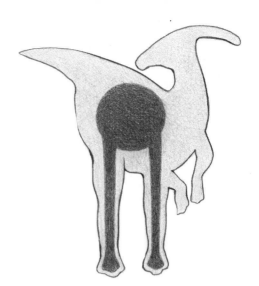

The limbs of all dinosaurs were upright (straight up and down), inserted under their bodies. Above is a bipedal dinosaur, *Parasaurolophus*. Below is a four-legged one, *Apatosaurus*. Notice the limb insertion is just like that of mammals.

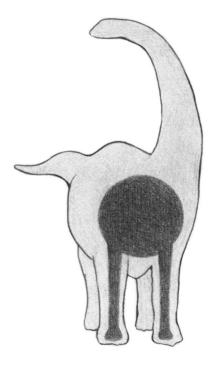

travels with its legs upright (although it certainly bends them), because they are inserted under its body, in the same way as those of the dinosaurs. Thus the dinosaur walk was mammallike. Dinosaurs did not crawl or creep along as reptiles do.

The upright leg posture of the dinosaur or mammal can only be achieved if the leg muscles stay tense, holding the body up. This, scientists tell us, requires a *high-energy* system. A high-energy system is one that takes in a great deal of food, has a great deal of internal chemical activity going on, and expends a great deal of energy. Such a system is found only in "warm-blooded" animals. Upright leg posture, therefore, goes together with "warm-bloodedness." This, in turn, strongly suggests the dinosaurs of the past were "warm-blooded."

(2) The fossilized skeletons of dinosaurs show that the *length* and *proportion* of their *leg bones* were not like those of reptiles. They were like those of mammals. Reptiles, if they have legs, have short ones. This is especially true for big reptiles. The dinosaurs, however, had long legs.

More importantly, the proportions of many dinosaurs' legs suggest that they were speedy animals. You see, the lower part of their legs, from the knee to the

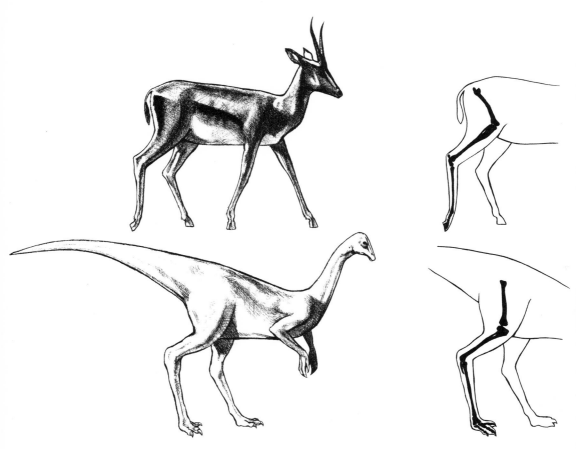

Ornithomimus had the leg proportions of a speedy animal.
Notice the similarity in the length of the limb bones of
Ornithomimus to those of today's gazelle.

foot, was quite long in some dinosaurs. Animals that
have this trait are almost always very fast runners. The
modern gazelle, for example, has lower leg bones that
are longer than its upper ones. Gazelles are extremely
swift animals. Surprisingly, some dinosaurs, such as

Ornithomimus (a two-legged, ostrich-sized saurischian), had leg bones with proportions just like those of the gazelle. This suggests that they were extremely swift too.

Although many reptiles are quick in short bursts, they do not have the ability to travel great distances quickly because they don't have the high-energy system needed for such a feat and because they don't have the right kind of limbs. Since dinosaurs such as *Ornithomimus* did have the right kind of limbs, it seems they were able to travel far and fast at the same time. This is a feat we expect from a "warm-blooded" animal having a high-energy system.

The largest known dinosaur, *Brachiosaurus*, held its head 40 feet (12 m) above the ground and weighed 80 tons.

(3) Most dinosaurs were *too big* to have been "cold-blooded." Reptiles, as we know, are "cold-blooded." Their blood, however, is not actually cold. They, like mammals, need their insides warm. They get them warm by basking in sunlight or by spending time in warm places. Of course their inside temperature goes up and down as the temperature around them goes up and down.

An animal as large as the very huge dinosaurs would be faced with an impossible task trying to warm up in the same way as a reptile. Scientists have shown that an animal weighing 10 tons would have to bask in the hot sunlight for 86 hours straight in order to raise its temperature inside just 1°C. The sunless nights in many regions of the world during the dinosaur age were cool. Also, by the middle of the Cretaceous period of the later dinosaurs, seasonal changes were occurring, so that any 10-ton "cold-blooded" animal would have been threatened often by the danger of losing some of its body warmth. But if a 10-ton "cold-blooded" animal's inside temperature dropped only 1°C, it would need 86 hours of continuous sunlight to bring it back up. Of course it could not get it, simply because the sun doesn't shine at night. (Even if it could somehow get that much sunlight, the temperature on its surface would become painfully high. It would burn the hide and probably kill the animal before any of the heat would penetrate the insides of the animal to warm them up.) All of this shows us that a 10-ton animal could not get its body warmth in the manner that reptiles do. It is simply too big for the sun to affect its internal temperature. And remember, scientists say a 10-ton animal is too big—think what this means for the *80-ton Brachiosaurus*.

MacRMoni
and Chese
Boil noodles
Chese and
noodle mix
Together.

(4) Fossilized dinosaur *bones* show that they had many *blood vessels* (called Haversian canals) running through them. We find these today in most mammals' bones. They are not something we expect to find in reptiles' bones.

These blood vessels in the bones serve important tasks. One of the most important is that they allow the

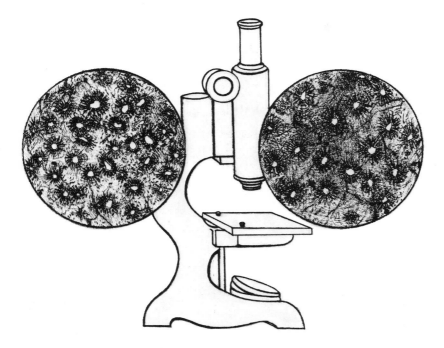

Dinosaur bones generally were filled with many blood vessels, called Haversian canals. To the left is pictured a slice of mammal bone, to the right is a slice of dinosaur bone. Their similarity suggests a similarity in calcium requirements.

muscles to get calcium from the bones. The calcium is needed by the muscles. Without it, they cannot work.

High-energy animals use their muscles a great deal. Therefore, as we might expect, they need plenty of calcium sent to their muscles and they have the many blood vessels in their bones to supply this calcium. Reptiles, however, usually do not need much calcium sent to their muscles. So they do *not* need many blood vessels in their bones.

(5) The number of dinosaur predators, compared to the number of dinosaurs that were prey, was small. This seems to mean *each dinosaur predator ate a great deal*. This is unlike any reptile.

Although it may surprise you, reptiles do not eat very much. Even the Komodo Dragon, the largest monitor lizard in the world today, eats far less than any mammal of the same size. Scientists have shown that it takes the Komodo Dragon 60 days to eat an amount of food that equals its own body weight. In contrast, a lion of the same size may eat its own body weight in food in only 8 days.

Because the dinosaurs that were predators seem to have eaten a great deal, it appears they were "warm-blooded" animals needing plenty of food for energy, as a mammal does.

(6) The fossilized skeletons of dinosaurs show that dinosaurs had *secondary palates* (a shelf of bone and tissue) inside their mouths. Reptiles do not (although crocodiles do have roofs to their mouths that resemble secondary palates).

Secondary palates are important. They separate, on the inside, nostrils from the mouth. This allows an animal to breathe while its mouth is filled with food. Because they do not have secondary palates, reptiles cannot breathe while they eat. But they don't need to, for they do not require a constant supply of oxygen. Mammals, however, (except for marine mammals such as whales) do require a constant supply of oxygen.

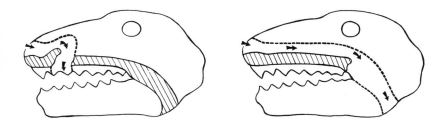

Pictured above left is a reptile head showing the typical reptilian mouth: air enters through the nostrils into the front of the mouth. Above right is a mammal head showing the typical mammalian mouth with its secondary palate. Because of the secondary palate, air that comes through the nostrils enters well in back of the mouth. This allows the animal to breathe even when the mouth is full of food. The secondary palate is also a dinosaur characteristic.

Their high-energy systems need plenty of oxygen to "burn" the calories in their food, thereby turning it into fuel. So mammals need secondary palates and, of course, have them.

Since dinosaurs had secondary palates, we must guess that they also required a constant supply of oxygen, even while eating. This is not true of reptiles.

All of these differences put together make a strong case. It certainly does seem that dinosaurs of the past were not reptiles. In fact, the evidence we have just examined places dinosaurs closer to mammals than to reptiles! But we cannot call dinosaurs mammals either: We have no proof that any dinosaur had milk-secreting glands, which an animal must have to be a mammal. Too, we know that fossilized dinosaur skulls are not like those belonging to mammals. Dinosaur skulls, you may recall, are reptilelike. Also like reptiles, dinosaur teeth were constantly replaced throughout their lives.

Then what were the dinosaurs? Were they reptiles or were they mammals? We must answer that they were neither. The dinosaurs of the past were in a class by themselves. Nevertheless, almost all taxonomists still place them in the class named *Reptilia*. This clearly seems to be a serious mistake. Some paleontologists (scientists who study fossils) have suggested a

way to correct it. They say dinosaurs must be taken out
of the *Reptilia* class and put into a new one, named
Dinosauria.

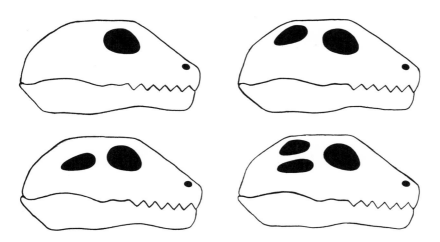

The number and placement of openings in the skull give us four
basic types. Top left is the *anapsid* skull having no openings
beyond those of the eyes and nostrils. This is typically an
amphibian and turtle skull.

Top right is the *euryapsid* skull, having one opening placed
high in back of each eye. This type is found in the extinct
plesiosaurs.

Bottom left is the *synapsid* skull, having one opening placed
low in back of each eye. This type is found in the ancestors to
all mammals, the therapsids, and in mammals themselves.

Bottom right is the *diapsid* skull, having at least two
openings (in addition to those for the eye and nostril) placed in
each side. This type is found in reptiles, pterosaurs, and
dinosaurs (including birds).

A few daring scientists also want *birds* to be included in this new class named *Dinosauria*. This is because they believe that birds are dinosaurs. To learn why they believe this, we must examine the evidence they have gathered to prove their claim.

Are Birds Dinosaurs?

At the present time, birds have their own class, named *Aves*. They have their own class because only they have feathers. Is this enough to get a class all by themselves? Perhaps it is. But if another kind of animal should turn up with feathers, we would have to question whether or not birds really do deserve their own class. Well, this is precisely what has happened. That "other kind of animal" turned up in the form of a fossilized skeleton of an animal named *Archaeopteryx*.

Almost from the moment the first fossilized skeleton of *Archaeopteryx* was discovered in 1862, the animal has been the subject of scientific debate. Through the years, people have called it a feathered lizard, a "griffin," a bird, and a dinosaur. One look at this

Although its feathers make it appear airworthy, *Archaeopteryx* was not a flyer.

strange, crow-sized animal's skeleton and we can see why: *Archaeopteryx* was covered with feathers, it had sharp teeth, a pointed snout, a long bony tail, and three clawed fingers near the end of each of its two wings.

Surely this was a perplexing animal. The debate over exactly what it was went back and forth until it seemed to rest on the side that called it a bird. Those who believed *Archaeopteryx* was a bird based their argument on the fact that it had feathers. They also pointed out that its bones were hollow like birds' bones, and that it had large orbits (holes for the eyes) in its skull, as birds do. And, finally, they based their argument on the fact that *Archaeopteryx* had a collarbone (a "fused" one, called a furcula, or wishbone).

You see, it was believed that no dinosaurs had collarbones.

The people who believed *Archaeopteryx* was a
bird were winning the debate until 1973. In that year
an American geology professor named John Ostrom
discovered, by looking very carefully, that some dino-

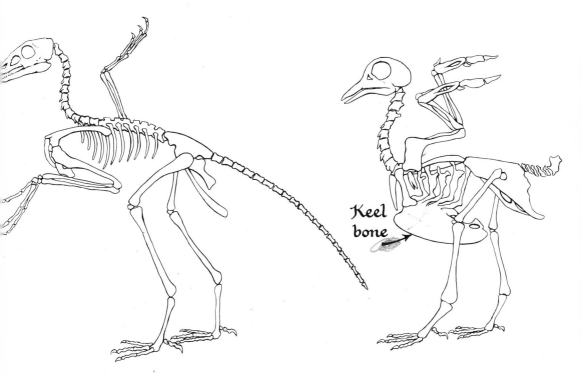

Keel
bone

Although *Archaeopteryx* was feathered and had large holes in its
skull for its eyes, its skeleton overall was different from a typical
modern bird skeleton. Notice *Archaeopteryx* did not have the
"keel" bone found in birds of flight.

saurs *did* have collarbones. This meant that *Archaeopteryx* could have been a dinosaur.

Professor Ostrom's additional work seemed to show that *Archaeopteryx* was indeed a dinosaur. It was a coelurosaur, a small, bipedal (two-legged), speedy predator-scavenger placed in the *Saurischia* order. Professor Ostrom discovered the following interesting things about *Archaeopteryx:*

(1) It did not have the ability to fly, because it did not have a breastbone, nor the proper forearm bones, nor the proper shoulder socket. It also did not have enough muscle (we know this because muscles leave scars on bones where they connect, and *Archaeopteryx*'s bones show few scars), and it was probably too heavy (with its long bony tail and many teeth) to fly.

(2) It did not have the sturdy "undercarriage" necessary to land safely, even if it could have somehow become airborne. Unlike the modern bird's pelvic bones, those of *Archaeopteryx* were not joined together to form one strong bone. So they probably could not have taken the shock of landing.

(3) Its elbow, wrist, and fingers were not joined together. Those of modern birds are.

Archaeopteryx was very similar in body form to other coelurosaurs that lived at the same time. The silhouette of *Archaeopteryx* (left) alongside that of *Compsognathus* (right) shows that the greatest difference was in the arms: *Archaeopteryx* had especially long ones.

In showing us how unlike a modern bird *Archaeopteryx* was, Professor Ostrom showed us, at the same time, that its skeleton was just like a coelurosaur's. In fact, if we take away the feathers, the skeleton *is* that of a coelurosaur. What we have, then, is the fossilized skeleton of a feathered coelurosaur. But it was no ordinary one, for it was well on the way to becoming what we call today a bird. After all, it did have many characteristics of our modern birds.

Whether *Archaeopteryx* is called a dinosaurlike bird or a birdlike dinosaur is not especially important. But it is important that we understand that *Archaeopteryx* represents the beginning of the avian, or bird, life forms. (Recently, however, a single birdlike bone has been found in Colorado, which may belong to a dinosaur that lived before *Archaeopteryx* did. New discoveries usually bring new questions.)

Being able to trace modern birds back to their origin helps us understand them better. Birds are "warm-blooded" creatures. But it was thought that they were very closely related to reptiles. This idea is finally being overturned. Coming in its place is the idea that the "warm-blooded" birds of today evolved directly from "warm-blooded" animals of the distant past, the dinosaurs.

Of course, knowing that birds evolved from coelurosaurs helps us understand the extinct dinosaurs better too. We can look to birds and listen to them too, to get good strong hints about what the dinosaurs of millions of years ago were like.

Archaeopteryx was a birdlike dinosaur that could not fly. Then what was the purpose of its feathers? Scientists agree the feathers on *Archaeopteryx* served at least one important duty: They kept the animal warm. Feathers served *Archaeopteryx* just as fur serves mammals—they provided *insulation*.

Archaeopteryx needed some form of insulation because it was a small (crow-sized) animal. All small "warm-blooded" animals need insulation, because their tiny bodies are very sensitive to heat and cold. Without insulation they would easily lose their internal body warmth, and they would easily become very cold. In contrast, very large animals can hold their internal body warmth well, and they do not become very cold so easily. (Perhaps we should keep in mind that there are different kinds of insulation. Human beings, for example, do not have fur, nor do we have much hair. And we certainly don't have feathers. Our forms of insulation are our clothes and heated homes. Other "hairless" mammals must solve the problem in a similar way or grow to a very large size, like an elephant. Usually, burrowing into a hole provides a warm home. Mammals of the cold seas, of course, have great amounts of fat for insulation.)

Its feathers also prove that *Archaeopteryx* was "warm-blooded": Feathers not only protect the animal from low temperatures, they also protect the animal from hot sunlight. Because of this they would make it extremely hard for an animal to get its insides warmed up by sunlight. Feathers, therefore, would probably never be found on a "cold-blooded" animal.

It makes good sense that feathers evolved to serve as insulation for small dinosaurs such as *Archaeopteryx*. But we are perplexed about one thing: It is a long way from insulation to flight. Why did the feathers evolve all the way to become wings? They might easily have remained short and served well as insulation, but they didn't. It seems they must have been useful for something in addition to insulation. Two ideas have been offered, and scientists do not agree on which is correct. Some believe the feathers were used in gliding. They point out that the tail feathers resemble the design of the tails of some modern gliding mammals. These scientists suggest that *Archaeopteryx* climbed trees to become airborne.

Others disagree. They point out that *Archaeopteryx* would not have survived landing because its "undercarriage" was not strong enough. They also say the feathers of *Archaeopteryx* were not inserted deeply enough to have been very strong. (Feathers must be firmly inserted to resist winds if they are to be useful for flight.) The scientists on this side of the debate believe that *Archaeopteryx* used its feathers like a butterfly net, to catch insects. This may be the correct answer, for *Archaeopteryx* does not appear to have been an airworthy animal. However, unless more evidence is found in the fossil record, the debate will probably continue.

Another debate about feathers concerns other small dinosaurs that lived alongside *Archaeopteryx*. Since they were small, we would expect that they too needed insulation. Recently some paleontologists claimed they *have* seen feathers in the fossils of *Comp-*

Archaeopteryx probably used its wings to capture insects.

sognathus, a two-foot (60 cm) coelurosaur. But not all scientists agree feathers are there. Perhaps future discoveries will eventually settle this question.

Compsognathus was a small coelurosaur, measuring 2 feet (.6 m) from head to tail. Some paleontologists believe *Compsognathus* was feathered, for feathers would have been useful as insulation on so small an animal. Most paleontologists, however, believe *Compsognathus* was featherless.

The great luck of the coelurosaurs in evolving feathers enabled them to eventually conquer the air. Birds were numerous and successful by the end of the Mesozoic era, around 65 million years ago. Their success, of course, continues to the present day. From this single line of dinosaurs there are today over 8,600 species of birds.

Dinosaurs and Their World

Thanks to our new understanding of *Archaeopteryx*, it is proper to think of the many birds on earth today as a line of dinosaurs, the coelurosaurs. Studying birds can surely give us clues about what dinosaurs of the distant past were like. But birds cannot give us an idea of how very different the various dinosaurs were from each other. Nor can birds tell us much about the world of the dinosaurs.

The dinosaur world was mostly a warm, wet one, with a *stable climate*, meaning there was no drastic change in weather or temperature. But gradual changes did occur, both before and during the "age of the dinosaurs."

Just before the first dinosaur existed, the world

was quite wet and fairly warm. Then, around 225 million years ago, things became even warmer, but many of the wetlands and swamps dried up. Millions of years later, by 175 million years ago, the world was somewhat wetter again, and the plant life lusher.

With the coming of the Cretaceous period, about 135 million years ago, the world became still wetter and a bit cooler, and the lowlands became covered with seas. By the middle of the Cretaceous period, seasonal weather was occurring, so much of the earth's animal and plant life was experiencing, for the first time, low temperatures brought on with each "winter" season.

While these changes in climate were occurring, something else of great importance was happening: *The continents were forming.* When the Triassic period began about 225 million years ago, there were no

Two hundred and twenty-five million years ago the continents we know today were joined together, forming one vast supercontinent, named Pangaea. Two hundred million years ago Pangaea began to split in two, forming one large land mass named Laurasia in the north, and one large one in the south, named Gondwanaland. By the end of the Cretaceous period, 65 million years ago, our modern continents had formed from these two splitting apart. Evidence shows our continents continue to move, and they seem to be moving at a pace equal to that of the land masses of 200 million years ago.

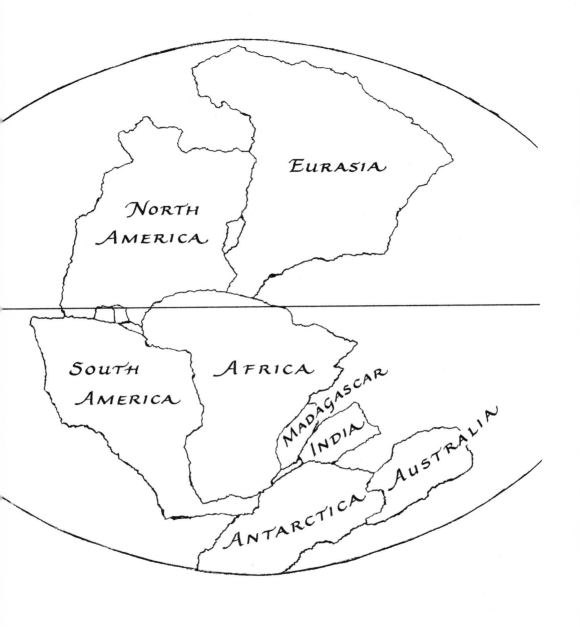

oceans between continents. In fact, the continents we know today were connected then, forming one great supercontinent. Scientists call the supercontinent *Pangaea*. Almost 200 million years ago Pangaea began to split apart, but very slowly. By the time the Cretaceous period was ending, around 65 million years ago, the continents had formed out of Pangaea: North America had split from South America; South America had split from Africa; India had split from Australia and Antarctica; and Madagascar broke away from Africa.

Back when the continents were joined together as Pangaea, the dinosaurs, in a span of less than 20 million years, spread throughout the land. When the continents did form, the dinosaurs, of course, became separated.

As geographic changes occurred, changes also took place in the plant life. For example, as the Cretaceous period neared its end, flowering plants became abundant. Also, temperate climate trees such as oak, maple, walnut, poplar, and hickory showed up in the Northern Hemisphere. Before this had happened there were only spore-bearing plants such as ferns, and seed plants such as cycads, ginkgoes, and conifers.

Changes in their surroundings resulted in changes in the dinosaurs. During their long "reign," the dinosaurs took many forms. Most taxonomists say there

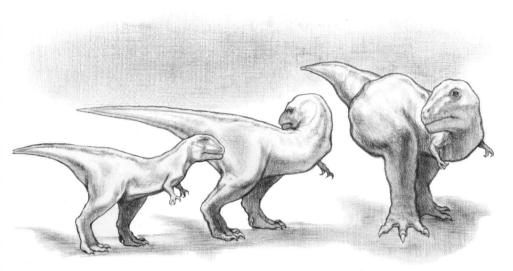

If we were to make a simplified judgement about dinosaur evolution we would be justified in saying that they became bigger and bigger until the mass extinctions at the end of the Cretaceous period. The carnosaurs demonstrate this well. *Teratosaurus* (left) was about 20 feet (6 m) long and weighed just under a ton. *Megalosaurus* (center) was about 25 feet (7.5 m) long and weighed from 2 to 5 tons. *Tyrannosaurus* (right) was about 30 feet (9 m) long and weighed 8 or 9 tons. *Teratosaurus* was a carnosaur of the Triassic period, *Megalosaurus* lived in the Jurassic period, and *Tyrannosaurus* lived in the Cretaceous period.

were over 500 different species of them. Their sizes and shapes varied a great deal, but mainly they became bigger and bigger. The carnosaurs (meat-eaters placed in the *Saurischia* order) illustrate this well, judging from *Teratosaurus* compared to *Megalosaurus* compared to *Tyrannosaurus*.

Tyrannosaurs were each about twice as large as a good-sized elephant, but the largest dinosaurs were the sauropods, the long-necked, long-tailed animals (also placed in the *Saurischia* order) most of us have seen in funny cartoons. All sauropods were probably plant-eaters, and the biggest of them, the brachiosaurs, were each as large as a herd of twelve or even fifteen elephants. Thus, we are talking about truly huge animals. Even though we have their fossilized skeletons to look at today, it is difficult to imagine such gigantic animals walking our earth. No doubt the first people who saw these skeletons had difficulty believing what they saw. They probably asked themselves how creatures of such great size lived. The scientist, however, also asks *why*.

In the last dozen years or so, a good solid answer has been given to the question of why dinosaurs were so big. The answer is fairly simple, and we have already been given a hint of it in our discussion of *Archaeopteryx*'s feathers. The feathers, remember, served *Archaeopteryx* as insulation. *Archaeopteryx* needed insulation because it was a small animal. With insulation it was able to hold its internal body warmth and survive any drop in temperature. Featherless dinosaurs had to face the same problem, and they solved it using a different method: Instead of insulation, they had great size. We have already discussed the fact that large bodies (whether they are of dinosaurs or not!) hold their internal temperature much better than small ones. The great dinosaurs, through evolution, took advantage of this principle. They became extremely large to hold their internal body warmth.

So, it was their hugeness itself that kept the huge dinosaurs warm. All the small "warm-blooded" animals in the dinosaur age had insulation (the mammals had fur, the smallest dinosaurs had feathers). These facts tell us there must have been a cooling trend in the climate that occurred over thousands and thousands of years.

Of course, dinosaurs did not all of a sudden decide to become larger and larger. The change occurred through evolution, and evolution is not something a life form can control. It is a two-step process involving genes (tiny units inside all life forms that transmit certain characteristics of parents to offspring) and the environment (the surroundings outside all life forms). The variety of life that we see is due to the remarkable ability of genes to combine in different ways to make up each living thing. Genes, therefore, not only cause offspring to resemble their parents; they also occasionally cause offspring to differ so much from their parents that whole new species can be created.

The survival of each living thing depends upon

how well it fits into its environment. Those that fit well survive, those that do not fit well do not survive. Any one of a number of factors could destroy the fitness of a living thing: Climate, soil, or water conditions may drastically change, a new enemy may appear that is impossible to defend against, a new, better equipped competitor for food may appear, or the food supply itself may disappear. Throughout Earth's history many living things reached a point at which they, for one reason or another, no longer fitted well into their environment and they became extinct because of it. Nature eliminated them, for, in the words of the scientist, "nature selects against a living thing that is not well-suited to its environment." (In fact, nature has eliminated 99.9 percent of all the species that have ever lived!)

Some dinosaurs must have been better suited under certain geographic and climatic conditions than others. We believe this because not all dinosaurs lived at the same time: As one kind would die out, another kind better suited would be there replacing it. Throughout the history of dinosaurs there were times when one kind was dominant, and then other times when another kind was.

It is significant that the coelurosaurs remained small throughout the dinosaur age. (They continued to

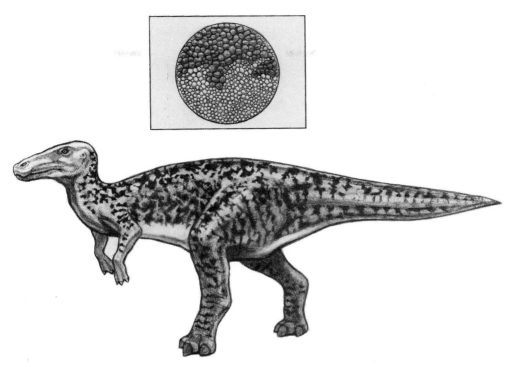

Fossilized skin of *Anatosaurus* shows that it was covered with small lumps called tubercles. The tubercles differed in size: The largest ones covered the animal's back and legs, while the smallest ones covered its belly. Scientists guess the size differences indicate differences in color. *Anatosaurus* (also named *Trachodon*) was a "duck-billed" dinosaur, 20 to 33 feet (6–10 m) long, weighing perhaps 5 tons.

be scavengers and predators all along.) Apparently they did not have to become large because they evolved into insulated (feathered) animals. Therefore, they were able to survive the cooling climate without becoming huge.

In addition to varying in size, dinosaurs apparently varied in color. A specimen of *Anatosaurus* (also named *Trachodon*) showing fossilized skin proves that it was covered with *tubercles,* or lumps, of different sizes. The largest tubercles were on the back and legs, while the smallest ones covered the belly. Because most animals known today have their undersides lighter in color than the rest of their bodies, scientists guess the size differences of the tubercles indicate differences in color.

Exactly what colors dinosaurs were we cannot say. If the colors served as camouflage they were probably various shades of green, for the world at that time was mostly a green one (from the abundant plant life). Or they might have been shades of brown, to match areas caused by dried plant life or patches of bare earth or rock.

If the colors served to help species identify themselves, or to help males and females tell each other apart, they could have been almost any color imaginable. Birds of today certainly are; especially those in tropical areas, which have climate and some vegetation similar to that of most of the dinosaur age.

The larger dinosaurs were probably less colorful than the smaller ones, if what we see before us today is a rule in nature: The largest birds are not so colorful as

Euparkeria was a bipedal, 3-foot (.9 m) pseudosuchian thecodont, ancestor to the dinosaurs and pterosaurs.

the smallest. And, too, all mammals of great size come in the "earth colors" of brown, pale yellow, or gray. None of these colors is very strong.

Whatever their color, there is a good possibility that at least some of the dinosaurs of the past were able to see colors. This is an exceptional ability, for most animals today see only shades of gray. Many modern birds, however, do see colors, and this gives us reason to suspect that their ancestors the coelurosaurs also did.

Although the dinosaurs did not actually "rule" the earth, they were the dominant large life forms of their time. Exactly when the first one came into existence is impossible say, because paleontologists do not agree about which animal was the first dinosaur. This is because the difference between an advanced *pseudosuchian thecodont* (the ancestor to the dinosaur) and a

Ornithosuchus seems to have been an animal in between: Some scientists call it a pseudosuchian thecodont, while others call it a dinosaur. It was 10 to 12 feet (3–3.6 m) long from head to tail and traveled bipedally.

One of the earliest true dinosaurs was *Coelophysis,* an 8 to 10-foot (2.4–3 m), 50 pound (23 kg) speedy coelurosaur.

primitive dinosaur is not especially clear. The argument over *Ornithosuchus* shows us this, for some scientists call it a pseudosuchian thecodont, while others call it a dinosaur. *Ornithosuchus* had a pelvis and limb structure that enabled it to travel bipedally, with its hind legs upright under its body. But the pelvis and limbs were not quite the typical dinosaur pelvis and limbs. They were not so perfectly placed for bipedal walking. This of course means *Ornithosuchus* was not able to walk so well in the bipedal position. It seems, therefore, to have been much like the pseudosuchian thecodonts in this respect, for the pseudosuchian thecodonts didn't travel as well on two legs as the dinosaurs precisely because they did not have the dinosaur pelvis and limbs.

There is agreement, however, that *Coelophysis*, a swift, bipedal predator placed in the *Saurischia* order, was among the earliest true dinosaurs. Another early one, also a saurischian, was *Thecodontosaurus*, a 10-foot (3 m) forerunner of the gigantic sauropods.

These animals lived almost 220 million years ago. Fifteen million years later, dinosaurs were the most numerous land animals of all. Well before the close of the Triassic period, the world was theirs. They went on to dominate it for almost 140 million years.

Sauropod Success

The sauropods seem to hold our attention and fire our imagination more than most other dinosaurs simply because they were the biggest. Yet there are other things besides their size that make the sauropods interesting. To begin with, there's the question of whether they lived in or out of water.

The scientists who first studied the fossilized skeletons of sauropods eventually came up with the idea that these animals spent most of their time in deep waters. The scientists guessed this was so because they believed the sauropods were too large to remain standing on land. It was assumed that the water buoyed up their heavy bodies and great tails.

Today we feel that this was not how sauropods

46

lived. They could not have spent much time in deep waters because the *water pressure* would have been too much for them. If we, in our imagination, place the sauropod *Diplodocus* in water deep enough so that it would have to "snorkel-breathe" for air, the water would be about 26 feet (7.9 m) deep. At this depth, the pressure of the water surrounding the chest of *Diplodocus* would prevent its lungs from expanding. *Diplodocus* simply would not be able to breathe. Also, the pressure of the water would probably crush *Diplodocus*'s trachea, or windpipe. So *Diplodocus* certainly could not have walked along the bottoms of deep bodies of water, snorkel-breathing.

Yet some paleontologists still believe that sauropods were semiaquatic like the modern hippotamus.

Diplodocus, although reaching a length of almost 90 feet (27 m), was a lightweight sauropod, weighing perhaps "only" 10 tons.

They point to how high the nostril holes were placed in the skulls of sauropods and claim this prevented water from getting into their noses. They also point to the famous fossilized footprints of a sauropod "swimming." This fossil was found in Texas. It shows only the tracks of a sauropod's front feet, except for one hind footprint. Paleontologists explain that the animal must have been paddling through water, occasionally using its front feet to push into the water's bottom to move itself along. The one print of its hind foot is where the animal kicked the bottom to change its direction.

A third reason why some paleontologists believe sauropods were semiaquatic is because they believe it was safer for the sauropods in water than on land where the great meat-eating carnosaurs roamed.

Not all paleontologists are convinced that these things prove sauropods were semiaquatic. In fact, some have put together evidence that tells us quite the opposite was true. They explain the following about sauropods:

(1) Their bones were hollow and lightweight. This is not something we would expect in semiaquatic animals.

(2) Their limbs and rib cages do not resemble those of a hippopotamus. The hippo has short limbs and a rib cage shaped like a barrel. Sauropods had somewhat long limbs shaped like pillars, or columns. Their rib cages were deep. The limbs and rib cages of the sauropods were very similar to those of modern elephants.

Comparing the shape of the body and limbs of the hippopotamus (left), the elephant (center) and the sauropod (right), we can readily see the hippo does not fit in: Its barrel-shaped body and short muscular limbs are unlike those of the land-dwelling elephant and sauropod.

(3) The feet of sauropods were not like hippos' feet. They were short, stumpy, and encased in fleshy pads, just like the feet of elephants.

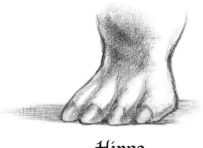

Hippo

The foot of the sauropod was encased in a fleshy pad, appearing remarkably like the foot of our modern elephant, except for a long-nailed toe or two, which the sauropod may have used for digging out plants. Notice the toes on the hippo foot: They can spread. This is useful for a semiaquatic animal that travels on water-softened earth.

Elephant

Sauropod

(4) The high nostrils do not prove that sauropods were semiaquatic. Many land animals have them. These holes placed so high in the skull might even be an indication of a proboscis, like that of an elephant or a tapir.

Did *Brachiosaurus* have a proboscis? The illustration of the brachiosaur skull shows how high the nostril holes were. Because of this, most paleontologists assume *Brachiosaurus'* nostrils were at the top of its head, as shown in the middle drawing.

However, there is the possibility that *Brachiosaurus* had a proboscis. The bottom drawing shows how *Brachiosaurus* might have appeared with a snout like that of a tapir.

(5) There is a lot of internal nasal development in sauropod skulls, indicating a keen sense of smell. Generally this is not something we would expect to find in a semiaquatic animal.

(6) Many sauropod fossils show severely worn teeth. What caused this? Most water plants are quite soft, and we have no evidence that leads us to believe sauropods ate anything like shellfish. We do know, however, that many *land* plants of the time were tough and abrasive: The coarse trunks of the palmlike cycads, the wood of the ginkgoes and conifers (redwoods, pine and fir trees), and conifer needles all might have served as food.

(7) The very long necks of sauropods suggest they were land animals: The hippo has a short neck. But the giraffe, for example, has a long one, which it uses to feed on tall trees, *on land*.

(8) The sauropod that went into water to escape from a carnosaur-predator made a deadly mistake. Carnosaurs such as *Allosaurus* were much better built for swimming than the sauropods were: Unlike the sauropods, *Allosaurus* had hind limbs that were built for speed and power. No doubt they would have served

Allosaurus (also named *Antrodemus* and *Labrosaurus*) was a large, powerful carnosaur, 27 to 36 feet (8.1–10.8 m) long and 2 to 5 tons in weight. Judging by its skeletal design, we may assume *Allosaurus* was able to travel fast on land—and quite probably in water too.

well for swimming, giving *Allosaurus* a powerful kicking stroke. The sauropods' columnlike legs, although immensely strong, were not designed to be useful for proficient swimming. If we judge by their skeletons, we must guess that the carnosaurs were superior swimmers. So the sauropods were safer on land.

In addition to these eight points, we have evidence that shows sauropods traveled in herds on land. For example, in Holyoke, Massachusetts, there is a fossil site of sauropod footprints making 28 trails. The footprints are of different sizes. All the large ones go in the same direction. This means the animals were not simply browsing. They were all heading for the same place.

All this evidence puts the sauropods firmly on land. This does not mean they never ventured into water. After all, we do have the trace fossil in Texas that shows that they probably did. But we must not say the sauropods were aquatic or semiaquatic just because of this fossil. For we know that elephants, for example, often go into water to cool down or to wash themselves; and they are neither aquatic nor semiaquatic animals.

The sauropod *Apatosaurus* (also named *Brontosaurus*) was 70 to 75 feet (21–22.5 m) long and weighed 30 to 40 tons.

The great size the sauropods attained has caused plenty of questions to be asked about their diet. We know that a large elephant of today eats, in the wild, about 300 pounds (136 kg) of vegetation each day. Some individual sauropods, as we have seen, were fifteen times as large as an elephant. Scientists wonder how such large animals found the massive amounts of food they must have required. It is also puzzling how they managed to eat large quantities of food, for their mouths were relatively small, and their teeth were not very well developed.

Scientists have found a fossilized skeleton of *Barosaurus* (a large sauropod with an especially long neck) with *gastroliths* very close by. Gastroliths are stones swallowed by an animal for the purpose of grinding up its food. They do the job of teeth, helping the digestion of food in the stomach. This means the sauropods, if they used stones in this way, were able to get the most out of their food. Still, they probably ate all day long.

Many people believe that the sauropods must have destroyed vast amounts of vegetation in their eating habits. Perhaps they did. But it can be said that an 80-ton sauropod would have been able to stay warm much more easily than 80 one-ton sauropods. So one would have required much less food than our imaginary 80

Diplodocus was capable of standing on its hind legs when it needed to.

smaller sauropods altogether would have required. This is because most of the food eaten by "warm-blooded" animals is used by their bodies just to keep them warm. Therefore, the hugeness of the sauropods, taking the weight of all the species put together, was favorable to the vegetation: thousands of tons of plant-eating dinosaurs in the form of very large animals would eat much less food than the same thousands of tons of plant-eating dinosaurs in the form of small animals.

Traveling in herds was also a lucky break for the vegetation: as a herd left an area to search for a new one with a fresh supply of vegetation, the old area's vegetation was given the chance to grow back. (No doubt a chance was all it needed: Growth must have been rapid, due to the generally warm and wet climate of the time.)

So, although we do not know how the sauropods managed to get their food, the amount they required was less than we might at first think; and it certainly was not too much for the earth to handle. The sauropods, after all, survived as a group for over 95 million years.

The fact that sauropods traveled in herds may mean that they did not lay eggs. If a baby dinosaur hatched from an egg, it had to be quite small. We know this because there is a limit to how large an egg can be. Scientists have estimated that an egg cannot be larger than about 24 inches (60 cm) in diameter. An egg any larger would have a shell too thick for the young animal to be able to break out of it. You see, the shell of an egg must be of a certain thickness in order to hold together. Therefore, a baby dinosaur would have had to fit into an egg no larger than one about 24 inches in diameter.

Scientists do believe that some dinosaurs did lay

eggs. We have fossilized eggs that appear to belong to nine different kinds of dinosaurs. (The eggs seem to have been like modern birds' eggs, not leathery like those of reptiles.) The largest eggs are about 10 inches (25 cm) in diameter, and scientists *think* they belong to *Hypselosaurus*, a sauropod. But how a baby sauropod only 10 inches long could have "kept up" with a moving herd of adults is a puzzle. Even if it could have somehow stayed with a moving herd, how it avoided being trampled is another. It is not likely a baby sauropod could have ridden on its mother's back, for it did not have grasping hands, and the shape of the body

The fossilized eggs found alongside the skeleton of *Hypselosaurus* are round, appearing very much like many modern birds' eggs. They were only 10 inches (25 cm) in diameter, while *Hypselosaurus* was a very large animal that often grew to be 40 feet (12 m) long.

Shown is a 36-foot (10.8 m) mother hypselosaur compared to a 20-inch (50 cm) baby. This is about the largest possible baby that could have hatched from an egg 10 inches in diameter (the baby would have had to have been tightly coiled inside the shell).

of the adult sauropod does not seem to have been suited for balancing young on top.

There is also the problem of growth. A mother crocodile, for example, lays very small eggs for an animal of her size. She may be as much as 2,000 times larger than her newly hatched baby. This means that her baby has a great amount of growing to do to reach adult size. But it surely isn't much compared to what a baby sauropod had to do—if baby sauropods came from eggs that were laid. The mother *Hypselosaurus* was 10,000 times larger than her baby, *if* those 10-inch-long eggs were hers. *Brachiosaurus*, the largest land animal we know of, was 100,000 times larger than her baby, if it came from a hatched egg. These figures make it hard for us to believe that sauropods laid eggs.

If a baby sauropod was born, and not hatched, what size was it at birth? How long did it take to grow to adulthood? Unfortunately, we do not have many fossils of young dinosaurs, and we do not have *any* of baby sauropods. Our questions cannot be answered unless we someday learn more from fossils.

Paleontologists have counted "growth rings" in the bones of the crests of ceratopsians (the four-legged "horned dinosaurs" placed in the *Ornithischia* order). It is believed that these rings may tell us how many years the animals lived, just as the growth rings in the

Recently bones were found in Colorado that appear to belong to a brachiosaur. However, they are about 25 percent *larger* than those of any known brachiosaur. Scientists have nicknamed the animal "Supersaurus". If it is a brachiosaur, Supersaurus may have weighed over 100 tons.

Pictured is Supersaurus superimposed on an average brachiosaur (in silhouette). The human silhouette shows how a 6-foot (1.8 m) man would have appeared alongside either animal.

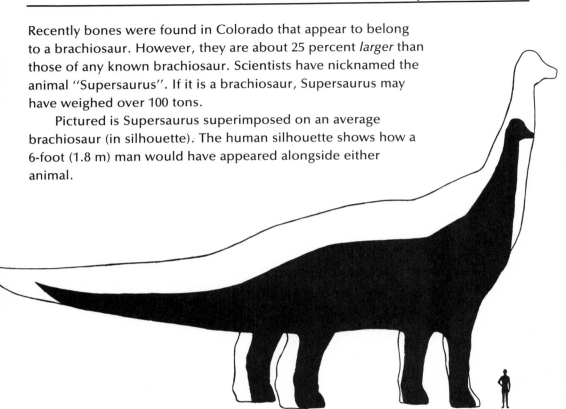

wood of trees tell us how long trees lived. Paleontologists have counted as many as 120 rings, so they believe the ceratopsians lived to be at least 120 years old. They further believe that the larger dinosaurs such as *Brachiosaurus* may have lived to be 200 years old. But these are only guesses. And even if they are right, they do not tell us how long it took for a baby to become an adult.

There were two types of heads among sauropods. Above is
Camarosaurus, with a deep skull; below is the rather flat-skulled
Diplodocus.

We are left with something of a mystery. Baby sauropods grew to be the largest animals in Earth's history
to walk the land. But we do not know just how they
came into the world.

Hadrosaurs: The Wary Giants

There is some mystery surrounding every dinosaur of the past. The "duck-billed" dinosaurs presented scientists with two of the very same problems as the sauropods. One dealt with the animals' habitat, the other dealt with their diet. The solutions to these problems provide us with an interesting account of the "duck-billed" dinosaurs, more properly called *hadrosaurs*. They are placed in the *Ornithischia* order, and developed almost 125 million years ago. Hadrosaurs are nicknamed "duck-billed" because of their snouts, which appear a bit like ducks' bills.

In addition to the "duck-billed" snouts, hadrosaurs had webbed hands, and most of them had crests on top of their heads. Some of the crests were truly

63

Parasaurolophus was a spectacular hadrosaur whose hollow crest occasionally reached a length of 7 feet (2.1 m)!

fantastic. Anyway, because of the snouts, webbed hands, and crests, people originally believed that these animals were aquatic. The crests, it was thought, were used for "snorkel-breathing" in deep waters. But this early guess was wrong. We know snorkel-breathing can be made impossible by water pressure. And in this case there was an additional problem. It had to do with the hadrosaurs' nostrils: They were not on top of their heads, but in the snouts, making snorkel-breathing quite impossible.

And although the hadrosaurs had webbed hands, they had *hooflike* feet! This suggests that hadrosaurs were land dwellers.

The snouts, in the fossilized skeletons, do outwardly resemble bills of ducks. On the inside, however, there's a big difference—teeth. Hadrosaurs, unlike ducks, had teeth. In fact, some had over two thousand of them! The teeth were prism-shaped, and

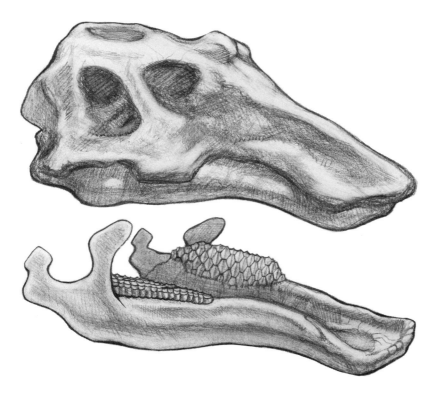

Pictured are the skull and lower jaw of *Prosaurolophus*. In the drawing of the lower jaw we can see the numerous, tightly arranged rows of interlocking teeth, which were typical of all hadrosaurs. Such teeth were highly efficient for both cutting and grinding.

he outside of the upper ones, and the inner sides
lower ones were coated with enamel. This al-
rough grinding surface to form on half of each
ooth where there was no enamel. All fossils show
teeth that are very worn, so hadrosaurs must have
eaten extremely tough, abrasive plants. It's hard to
imagine any water plants that might have been so
tough. However, there were many very tough *land*
plants abundant during the time the hadrosaurs
roamed the earth. There were the rough trunks of the
cycads, the woody parts of the ginkgoes and conifers,
and conifer needles. All might have formed part of the
hadrosaur diet.

We must conclude that the hadrosaurs were not
aquatic animals. No evidence exists that makes us believe they were.

By now you are probably wondering about the
crests. Certainly scientists have wondered about them
too. Indeed, most scientific investigation concerning
hadrosaurs has been of their crests. Actually, there are
in the fossil record two kinds of hadrosaurs: flat-
headed ones with no crests at all, and ones with crests
on their heads. The crested kind is further divided into
two types: hollow-crested and solid-crested. Often
people confuse the crested hadrosaurs with pachycephalosaurs. Both did have fantastic bone development

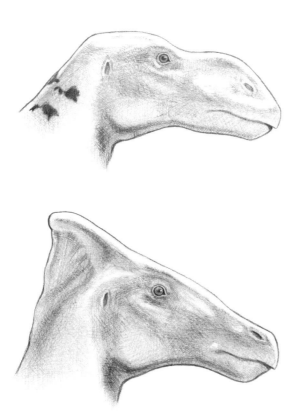

There were basically two kinds of hadrosaurs: flat-headed ones, and ones with crests on top of their heads. The crested hadrosaurs are further divided into two types: solid-crested, and hollow-crested. The top illustration is of *Kritosaurus,* a flat-headed hadrosaur; in the center is *Saurolophus,* a solid-crested hadrosaur; at bottom is *Corythosaurus,* a hollow-crested hadrosaur.

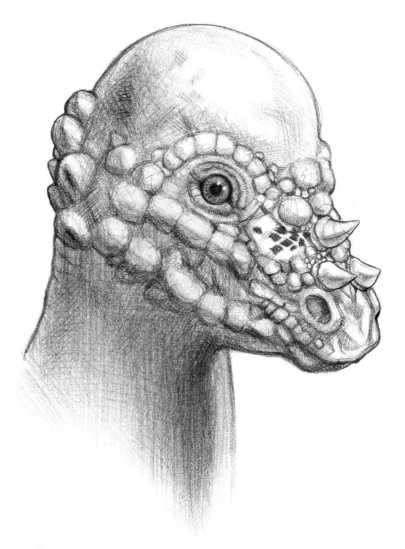

Pachycephalosaurus had a domed skull over 10 inches (25 cm) thick, with numerous large knobs of bone surrounding the dome. Paleontologists suspect pachycephalosaurs used their heads for butting, as wild sheep do today.

on the tops of their heads. But pachycephalosaurs were "dome-headed." Their skulls were extraordinarily thick. Some were over 10 inches (25 cm) thick! That was something far different from what the hadrosaurs had. (Pachycephalosaurs also had less developed teeth than hadrosaurs. Both pachycephalosaurs and hadrosaurs, however, are placed in the *Ornithischia* order.)

Originally it was thought that the hollow crests were used for snorkel-breathing. As we have seen, this idea is no longer accepted. Scientists now believe that the function of the hollow crests had to do with *smell*.

As far as we can tell, hadrosaurs were defenseless. (There is the possibility that they had a defense mechanism scientists cannot detect in their fossilized remains. For example, scientists could never tell if they had a defense system like that of the modern skunk.) If they *were* defenseless, they needed a keen ability to detect dangerous carnosaurs such as *Tyrannosaurus* that lived alongside them. Then they could immediately flee when carnosaurs came near. Just yet we are not sure of how good their hearing was, but the sense of smell in the hollow-crested hadrosaurs must have been extremely good, for their hollow crests were actually *nasal passages* that extended from their nostrils. They must have increased their sense of smell to a very high degree.

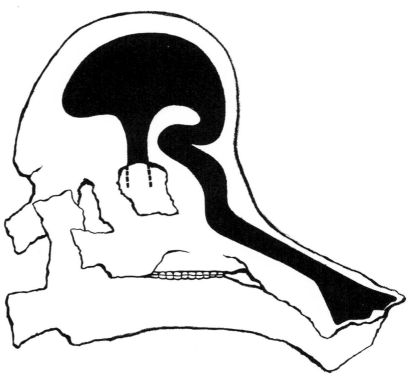

The darkened area in the skull of *Corythosaurus* represents the nasal passage that ran through the crest.

The idea of hadrosaurs standing upright on two legs to sniff the air for scents given off by dangerous predators intrigues paleontologists. They are intrigued by the possibility that dinosaurs gave off odors. What kind of odors they were we cannot tell. Did dinosaurs such as *Tyrannosaurus* sweat and secrete oils like those of mammals? Once again, we are left with unanswered questions.

Many paleontologists believe hadrosaurs also bellowed through their hollow crests. This would have been an added advantage, increasing the hadrosaurs' chances for survival, for it would have allowed them to communicate with each other over long distances.

The solid crests, of course, were not nasal passages, nor did they provide the hadrosaurs with sounding boards for bellowing. Paleontologists guess that the solid crests were used as modern wild sheep and goats use their horns: to fight duels by butting heads. Another guess is that they were used to butt attacking predators. But scientists have no evidence of these things, and we must remember that these crests were not nearly as thick as the pachycephalosaurs' domes. *Pachycephalosaurus* probably did use its dome as a battering ram, but this does not mean the solid-crested hadrosaurs also used their crests in that way.

Another guess about the solid crests is that they were for sexual display. By this it is meant that the crests made it easy for males and females to tell one another apart.

Finally, there is the possibility that the crests served to intimidate, or frighten, enemies. While scientists are not sure of what the function of the solid crests was, they do know the crests helped make hadrosaurs successful animals in their habitat, for these animals survived as a group for 60 million years.

Tyrannosaurus: The Waddling Killer

Tyrannosaurus may be the most famous dinosaur of all. For a long time now, it has been portrayed as a fearsome, ponderous predator. Usually it is shown walking upright, dragging its tail behind, always on the prowl. It has been called the largest carnosaur in Earth's history. However, recent work by scientists tells a different story. We have learned once again that some of our early ideas were wrong.

Tyrannosaurus certainly was a fearsome predator. Indeed, now that we know the way in which it moved about, it seems even more fearsome than we had guessed. _Tyrannosaurus_ did not run with its upper body straight up and down, but held it leaning far forward. It was almost perfectly horizontal. The tail did

Thirty feet (9 m) long and weighing 8 tons, *Tyrannosaurus* was a fearsome predator.

not drag along, but was off the ground, stretched out straight. The tail held in this way balanced the upper body, which leaned forward. Incidentally, it appears that hadrosaurs such as *Anatosaurus* moved along in this way too. They had support rods made of bone along their tails, keeping them rigid. We may also recall the fossilized trails of sauropods in Holyoke, Massachusetts. They show no trails left by dragged tails. Therefore, it seems that the sauropods also walked with their huge tails off the ground. This makes good sense: It prevented damage to the tails, for they might have easily been trampled if they were dragged along. An animal is slowed down by a dragging tail, so holding it off the ground allowed speedier travel.

Coming back to *Tyrannosaurus*, we must consider one more thing about its tail. The last 12 feet (3.6 m) of it that we usually see in illustrations or reconstructions have never actually been found in any fossil. The people who put them there did so because they guessed that was how the tail must have been. Some paleontologists, however, suggest the last 12 feet were never there in the first place. They believe *Tyrannosaurus* had a rather short tail, one that would have balanced the upper body better than a long one.

Along with its upper body held leaning forward, *Tyrannosaurus* waddled like a duck! We know this from studying the structure of the feet and lower limbs. You see, a group of strong tendons lined this area. With each stride *Tyrannosaurus* took, the tendons made the toes on the foot that was lifting off the ground clench, just as a modern bird's claw clenches on its perch. This allowed the foot to clear the ground. Also, the tail must have swung from side to side with each stride of the legs to balance the animal. Each leg also swung wide to take its stride, and all of this gave *Tyrannosaurus* a ducklike waddle.

Tyrannosaurus was probably also pigeon-toed. We have fossilized tracks of its near relative, *Megalosaurus,* and they show the toes pointing inward. It is likely that *Tyrannosaurus* walked in the same way. However, let's not make the mistake of picturing a pigeon-toed, waddling *Tyrannosaurus* moving along awkwardly and slowly. We know its prey moved along rather swiftly. Even the large ceratopsians (the four-legged "horned dinosaurs" placed in the *Ornithischia* order) probably traveled at speeds of up to 30 miles (48 km) per hour when they had to. With the leg proportions that *Tyrannosaurus* had, we assume it was able to catch much of its prey. We must also assume, however, that *Tyrannosaurus* tried for the easiest prey possible, as any good predator should. So it probably seldom— if ever—fought any healthy adult ceratopsians.

Tyrannosaurus was a remarkable killing machine. No doubt its great jaws were a formidable weapon. In addition to giving secure traction, the terrible claws on its hind legs were probably also used to tear flesh— they certainly appear deadly. But its front limbs are something of a puzzle. They were only 3 feet long (.9 m) and could not even have reached *Tyrannosau-*

Paleontologists believe *Tyrannosaurus* might have used its small but sturdy front limbs to brace itself as it used its massive hind limbs to push itself up from a lying position.

rus' mouth. So it is unlikely that they were used for feeding. Recently paleontologists have come up with an idea that explains their function. It is believed they were used to brace the body as *Tyrannosaurus* rose from a lying down position. This would explain why the end of each front limb had two clawed fingers, for they would have been used to dig into the ground as the hind legs pushed upward, Without them, it is believed, the animal would have simply slid forward along the ground. Along with this, *Tyrannosaurus* is believed to have sat with its legs tucked under itself, similar to the way a hen sits on its nest. *Tyrannosaurus* probably also rested its chest upon its front limbs, as a house cat does sometimes when it sleeps.

In 1965, an expedition in Mongolia found fossilized front limbs of a carnosaur that shocked paleontologists. The limbs resemble those of *Tyrannosaurus*, except they had three clawed fingers rather than two, and they were 8 feet (2.4 m) long. That is certainly much bigger than the 3-foot (.9 m) ones of *Tyrannosaurus*. Paleontologists have named this giant *Deinocheirus*. Unfortunately, none of its body has been found, so we do not know if it was a carnosaur that simply had very, very long front limbs, or was one built like *Tyrannosaurus*, but gigantic. In either case, *Deinocheirus* probably was a larger predator than *Tyrannosaurus*.

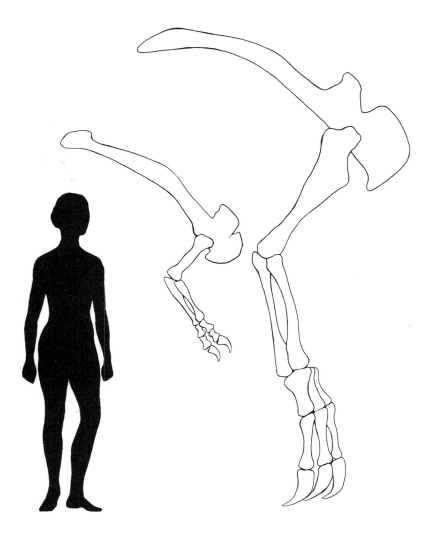

The front limb and hand bones of *Deinocheirus* (right) were much larger than those of *Tyrannosaurus* (center). The silhouette of the human figure shows how a person 5 feet, 4 inches (1.6 m) tall compares to the fossilized bones.

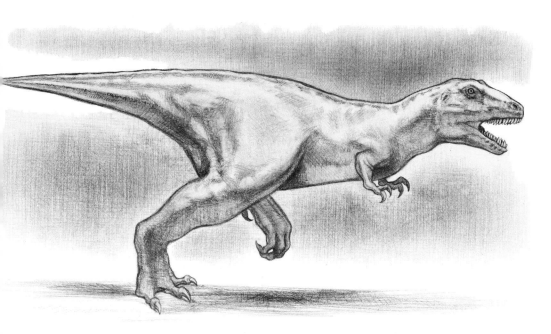

The charging tyrannosaur held its tail stretched out straight while its body leaned far forward.

This means we must hold back the title of "the largest carnosaur in Earth's history." We are not sure now what animal may have been the largest predator.

However, it is hard to imagine anything more fierce-looking than a charging tyrannosaur: the body pitched forward, aimed directly at its prey, the tail swinging violently from side to side as the great clawed legs waddled furiously, each claw digging into the earth for sure traction; and out in front of everything was the massive head, with its four-foot (1.2 m) jaws holding 60 six-inch (15 cm) daggerlike teeth. Surely *Tyrannosaurus* was eight tons of terror.

Pterosaurs:
Masters of Soaring Flight

Pterosaurs were not dinosaurs, although they did evolve from the same ancestors, the pseudosuchian thecodonts. Pterosaurs came about during the early part of the Triassic period, over 210 million years ago. Originally all pterosaurs were called "pterodactyls," and it was thought they were ancestors to our modern birds. We know today that this is not the case. There are differences in their skeletons (mostly in the pelvic region) that tell us they evolved separately from one another. (Birds, as we have seen, evolved from coelurosaurs.) However, pterosaurs were faced with the same problems that most of our birds are faced with today, and they solved them in much the same way. These problems dealt with *flight*.

Flying requires special equipment. A flying animal has a great need for high energy, and it must be light in weight. A flying animal faces problems of exhaustion and overheating, as well. Modern birds of flight solved all of these problems with one solution: *Their bones are hollow and have small openings in them that contain air sacs.* As a flying bird flaps its wings it breathes in air, much of which goes to fill the sacs. So the sacs are like balloons. With each wingbeat the air-filled sacs act like bellows, expanding and contracting. The lungs of birds are stiff, and these air sacs inside the bones help the lungs supply the body with oxygen. The great air flow from them also cools the body. The hollowness of the bones also means birds are light in weight.

Pterosaurs solved the problems in exactly the same way. By comparison, however, their bones were much thinner and more delicate than those of birds.

The brains of pterosaurs were also similar to those of modern birds. A bird's brain (and a mammal's brain) completely fills the "braincase" inside the skull. This is not the case with a reptile's brain. But it was the case with the pterosaurs.

The brain of a bird is also *shaped* differently than a reptile's brain, because different parts of it have become well developed. This happened because certain parts of an animal's brain deal with certain tasks the animal performs. The areas of the brain that deal with sight and coordination are highly developed in today's birds, for they have used their eyes and their coordination very much in flight. In contrast, the area of their brain that deals with smell is tiny ("underdeveloped") because they have not used (or needed!) their sense of smell very much. Fossils of the brains of pterosaurs have been pieced together. We have found that they were shaped just like those of modern birds.

It should come as no surprise that pterosaurs resembled birds of today so much, for they do share the same distant ancestor, the pseudosuchian thecodont. And the fact that birds, actually a line of dinosaurs, were mistakenly thought to have evolved from pterosaurs shows us how closely related all these animals are to each other.

Pterosaurs, then, were winged animals that were similar in many ways to flying birds of today. But there were important *differences* too. One difference was the way in which they flew. Birds that fly flap their wings. The early, small pterosaurs apparently did so too, though they did not do it as powerfully as the birds do. Pterosaurs, however, did not continue to evolve as flappers. Instead, through evolution, they went in another direction and used a different method of flying: They *glided*. Gliding, or soaring, was a perfectly good way to fly during most of the Mesozoic era, because the skies were calm. Pterosaurs apparently were master gliders, becoming the largest animals ever to have traveled through the sky.

The great *Pteranodon* is as interesting an example of a pterosaur as we could imagine. Its name means

Pterosaurs were not well suited for land travel. This illustration shows how two specimens of *Pteranodon* might have appeared while at rest on land.

"winged-toothless," and that's exactly what it was. Its proportions are startling: It had a 23-foot (7 m) wingspan, with a body the size of our modern turkey! It weighed somewhere between 20 and 40 pounds (9–18 kg), had spindly legs, and, of course, very thin-walled, hollow bones.

Thin-walled bones suggest *Pteranodon* was a glider, for flapping would have probably required more heavily-built bones in an animal so large.

The very light weight of *Pteranodon* also suggests that it was a glider. Indeed, *Pteranodon* was so light it must have been a supreme glider, as easily lifted as a sheet of paper. It has been estimated that a breeze less than 15 miles (24 km) per hour would have launched *Pteranodon* into the sky. *Pteranodon* would only have had to stretch its wings and the breeze did the rest. Only some very lightweight insects surpass *Pteranodon* in the ratio of body weight to wingspan.

In the sky, *Pteranodon* had a very low sinking speed, lower than today's human-made gliders. *Pteranodon* might have also had a membrane that extended from a bone on the wing finger (called a "pteroid bone") to its neck. This membrane would have acted like a parachute for gentle landing; yet it also would have aided in a takeoff, by trapping breezes under the animal.

Whether or not *Pteranodon* had such a membrane (not everyone agrees it did), *Pteranodon* was able to decrease its speed with its *swing-back wings*. If it found itself gliding too fast, or in a dangerous air current, *Pteranodon* was able to swing its wings backwards into a V shape. This decreased its speed by lessening its wing area and changing the flow and pressure of the air around its wings and body. (It increased what scientists call "drag due to lift.") It is interesting that this swing-back principle is the same one used

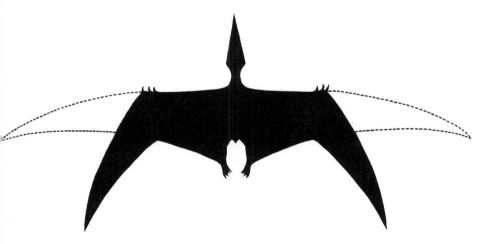

Flying speed depends upon numerous factors, but one of the most important is wingspan. *Pteranodon* was able to bend back its wings to form a V shape while in flight. This reduced its wingspan and therefore slowed down its flying speed. In this way *Pteranodon* was able to regulate its rate of travel through the sky.

today by "swing-wing," or "swept-wing," jet aircraft. (However, "swing-wing" jet aircraft travel at supersonic speeds. At such high speeds the forces that affect air travel—such as air pressure and air flow—act differently. Reducing the wingspan at supersonic speeds, in fact, allows for *faster* travel. So supersonic jet aircraft swing back their wings for a reason opposite to that of *Pteranodon*: they do it for increasing speed, not for slowing down.)

The bony crest on *Pteranodon's* skull is worthy of special attention. The crest at first may confuse us, for it appears heavy, and that would not seem to have been helpful to an animal built for lightweight gliding. But the function of the crest solves our puzzle: it held the body horizontal while *Pteranodon* was in flight. Also, when *Pteranodon* wanted to decrease altitude, it pointed its beak downward. When it did this, its crest of course pointed upward. In this manner the crest compensated for, or balanced, the weight of the beak. This held the head and body steady.

The crest also *saved* weight. Instead of having muscles to keep the head steady in the air, *Pteranodon* had its crest. The weight of the crest balancing the weight of the beak held it upright. The muscles that would have been needed to do this job would have weighed much more than the crest.

The large pterosaurs were probably "perpetual gliders," coming onto land very seldom, perhaps only to breed. Paleontologists believe this because the great pterosaurs' hind limbs do not appear to have been good for walking on land. Also, the flexible joint on each wing was about halfway from each end, so that its wingtips pointed toward the sky when the animal was on land, making for an awkward stance.

The small pterosaurs had similar disadvantages for walking on land. Paleontologists do not believe that they stayed floating on air like the large ones, so one guess is they must have lived like most bats do today. Sleeping in caves and hanging upside down from high places would have kept them safe from dangerous predators.

In addition to their method of flying and their inadequate ability to walk, pterosaurs differed from birds by having *fur* rather than feathers.

As long ago as 1901, a British geography professor named Harry Govier Seeley claimed, after carefully studying their fossils, that pterosaurs were "warm-blooded" and covered with some form of insulation. But he never found proof of his claim. His work was not accepted very well, and it only caused scientists to argue about what pterosaurs were and how they lived.

Through the years since 1901, a couple of paleon-

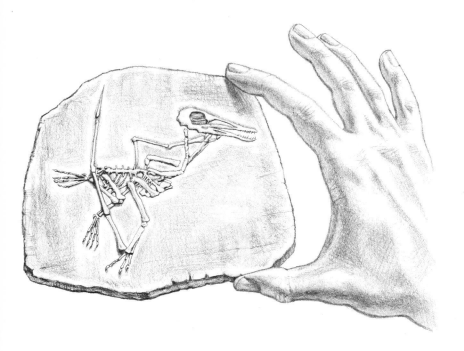

Small pterosaurs such as *Pterodactylus* probably flapped their wings. However, their ability to move about on land was not much better than that of the large pterosaurs. Pterodactyls varied in size: Some were not much larger than a hummingbird, others reached the size of a modern pigeon.

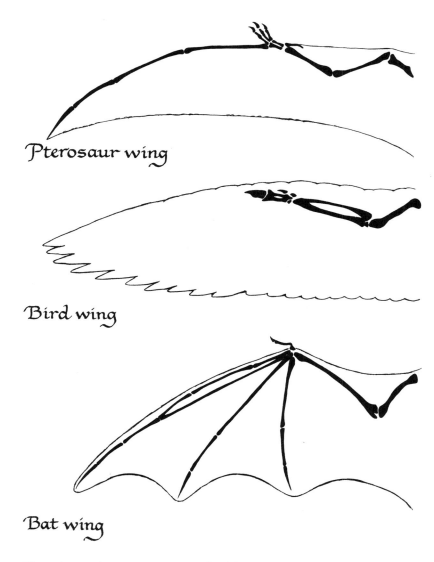

Pterosaur wing

Bird wing

Bat wing

The wings of pterosaurs were batlike: Rather than feathers, they were formed by skin that extended to the bones of the arm and fingers. Birds' wings are formed by feathers surrounding the "fused" arm and finger bones.

In 1970, fossil remains of *Sordes pilosus* ("hairy devil") were found, proving pterosaurs were fur-covered animals. *Sordes pilosus* was a small, early pterosaur that was part of a group named *Rhamphorhynchoidea*.

tologists did claim to see traces of fur in pterosaur fossils, but they were not believed. Then, in 1970, a Soviet paleontologist named A. G. Sharov discovered in the Soviet Union a very good fossil specimen of a small pterosaur. It clearly showed impressions of *soft, fleecy fur*. Professor Sharov named the animal *Sordes pilosus*, which means "hairy devil." This discovery not only settled the debate over whether or not pterosaurs had insulation, but it also proved once and for all that pterosaurs were "warm-blooded," for no "cold-blooded" animal would have insulation. Professor Seeley was right all along.

The diet of pterosaurs also causes a good deal of discussion among scientists. The small pterosaurs probably ate mostly insects. The large pterosaurs were fish-eaters. *Pteranodon* had a neck pouch like that of the modern pelican, and at least one fossil shows two species of fish caught in one of these pouches.

But it is puzzling just how *Pteranodon* caught fish. It could not have tucked its great wings against its body, for the wing had no ball-and-socket joint, which is necessary to do that. Therefore, *Pteranodon* could not have dived into the water as the pelican does. (To do so without tucking in the wings would break them!) Paleontologists also doubt that *Pteranodon* grabbed and held fish with its hind claws. The hind limbs do not appear to have been strong enough for that; and since they were so long, it probably would have upset *Pteranodon*'s balance if they were used in that way. So, paleontologists guess that a large pterosaur such as *Pteranodon* glided just above the surface of the waters and used its beak to snap up fish that swam close to the surface or jumped there.

Paleontologists assume *Pteranodon* glided just above the waterline in search of fish that swam at the surface or jumped out of the water.

Picturing *Pteranodon* gliding above the waterline in search of fish gives us a clue to its color. Birds that get their food in this manner almost always have their undersides colored white. The white color camouflages them against the sky so they are not so easily seen by the fish in the water. This principle is well-established in waterbirds and also in many marine animals that are predators. We assume it also worked for the large pterosaurs.

We can also be sure that the sun beating down on the back of a large pterosaur that was a "perpetual glider" could make it unbearably hot. One method of preventing heat absorption is through color. A dark color absorbs heat, a light one reflects it. To keep from overheating while soaring under the hot sun, the great pterosaurs needed to be very light in color. Therefore, scientists believe they probably were solid white! (Perhaps a few words on the polar bear's fur are necessary, for it might seem that a dark-colored fur would keep the polar bear warmer than the white fur it has. But this is not so, because polar bear fur is special. It acts not only as camouflage, but also to repel water and to *allow* heat to penetrate the skin. Each hair, you see, is hollow, and this allows light and heat to go right down through each one of them, all the way to the skin. Pterosaur fur, however, was soft and fleecy, quite unlike that of the polar bear. It therefore served the animal differently.)

The fur coat of the pterosaurs had to be kept clean, so pterosaurs must have been able to groom themselves. There was also the problem of raising young. Surely a very young pterosaur could not have glided for a long time in search of food. This means that pterosaurs were animals that cared for their young. Unfortunately, we have no fossil evidence that tells us how they raised their young, or where. Did they nest on offshore islands? Were they cliff-dwellers? As with the dinosaurs, scientists are left with many unanswered questions.

There also seems to be an unanswered question about how large a flying animal can be. Until 1972, scientists were sure that *Pteranodon* had become about as large as an animal could be and still fly. But in that year, fossil remains of a pterosaur were found in Big Bend National Park in Texas that had arm bones more than *twice* as large as those of *Pteranodon*. Paleontologists have named this tremendous animal *Quetzalcoatlus*, which comes from the Nahuatl language of the Aztecs of Mexico and was the name of their winged serpent god. The wingspan of *Quetzalcoatlus* is estimated to have been 50 feet (15 m) long.

It is puzzling that the fossil remains of this giant were found far from any body of water existing at that time. Furthermore, *Quetzalcoatlus* seems to have been similar to the type of pterosaur that had an extremely long neck. This has led some paleontologists to suspect that *Quetzalcoatlus* lived by scavenging dead dinosaur carcasses, and not by scooping up fish. However, this would have been a dangerous life, for the big ptero-

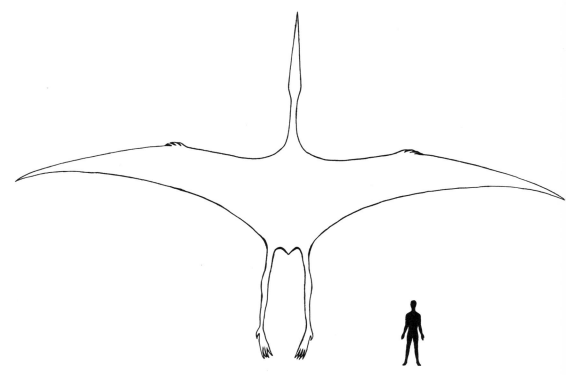

The largest pterosaur known, *Quetzalcoatlus,* may have had a wingspan of 50 feet (15 m). This drawing shows the great size of *Quetzalcoatlus:* The figure in silhouette is a 6-foot (1.8 m) tall man.

Pterosaurs and both orders of dinosaurs (saurischians and ornithischians) evolved from the same ancestor, the pseudosuchian thecodont. About 160 million years ago some coelurosaurs developed feathers, forming the line of dinosaurs we call birds. Coelurosaurs, feathered or otherwise, were theropods placed in the *Saurischia* order.

ERA PERIOD

MILLIONS OF YEARS AGO

CENOZOIC — Tertiary

65

MESOZOIC — Cretaceous

135

Jurassic

Birds

Pterosaurs   Saurischians   Ornithischians

195

Triassic

Pseudosuchian Thecodont

230

PALEOZOIC — Permian

280

saurs were awkward on land—and easy prey for the great carnosaurs. Until more evidence is found, we cannot say how *Quetzalcoatlus* got its dinner.

Although pterosaurs had fur and were therefore "warm-blooded," most taxonomists also continue to classify them as reptiles. This disturbs the paleontologists who believe that the pterosaurs were not reptiles at all. These paleontologists want the pterosaurs to get a class of their own, named *Pterosauria*. Taxonomists will eventually have to grant the wish of these paleontologists, for the fossil record proves that pterosaurs were no more like reptiles than mammals are.

Were Dinosaurs Stupid?

Human beings are animals that are often quick to call other animals stupid. Perhaps this is because we do not know of any other animals besides ourselves that have written books or have built great machines. Also, we believe we are the only animals that think deep thoughts. Although all these things are valuable for people to be able to do, they have not played a part in the evolution of any nonhuman animal. They have not been needed by any nonhuman animal for survival. So we must admit that they are not of value to nonhuman animals.

Nevertheless, scientists still seek to learn how smart each nonhuman animal is and this has always been a difficult problem. One reason for the difficulty

99

is that we do not completely agree on what "smart" or "intelligent" means. It is a very tricky thing, and people have not done well in explaining it. Many scientists believe that humans are smart because they have large brains and this has caused a great deal of study of the sizes of animals' brains.

The people who study brain sizes of animals do not only look for a big brain, they also look to find how large the different areas of the brain are. When the area of the brain that deals with sight is large, they assume it means keen eyesight for the animal. When the area of the brain that deals with smell is large, it means a good sense of smell, and so on. How large an animal's brain is and which areas are well-developed determine how smart or how stupid an animal may be.

Until recently, all dinosaurs were called stupid, because it was thought that they all had small brains. Today paleontologists know that this was not so. Coelurosaurs and dromaeosaurs (small, bipedal predators that descended from the coelurosaurs) had large braincases and the shape of their brains suggests that they were smart animals.

Pterosaurs, you may remember, had large brains that filled their braincases. Because of the size and shape of their brains, they too are considered to have been smart.

This leaves the large dinosaurs. They do seem to have had tiny brains. Does this mean that they were stupid? Before we make our guess, we should consider two things. First, there is size. Scientists have discovered that large animals have smaller brains in relation to their body size than small animals have, in relation to *their* body size. This means that an animal twice as large as another animal does *not* require a brain twice as large to do as well. Therefore, we would not expect a sauropod, that was, say, ten times the size of an elephant, to have had a brain ten times as large as an elephant's brain. We must keep this in mind.

The second thing that we need to consider is the fact that the large dinosaurs appear to have had tiny brains when compared to *mammals*. But when we compare them to *reptiles*, they do not seem so bad. Certainly they do not appear to have been simple, stupid beasts.

Either way, however, may not be fair to judge dinosaur smartness. The fact is dinosaurs were dinosaurs —they were not mammals or reptiles. We can say that brain size among dinosaurs *varied*, just as it does among mammals and among reptiles. Small dinosaurs such as the coelurosaurs had brains that were as well-developed as those of some mammals. The very large dinosaurs had brains that were about as developed as

Ornithomimus (also named *Struthiomimus*) was properly named "bird mimic" or "ostrich mimic." It clearly resembled the ostrich of today, standing 7 to 8 feet (2.1–2.8 m) tall and reaching as much as 14 feet (4.2 m) in length. *Ornithomimus* evolved directly from the smaller coelurosaurs but, unlike them, had no teeth.

some reptiles' brains. If brain size counts, we may guess that some dinosaurs were smart, and some were not. But we can only guess. All the studies of measurements and comparisons of brain sizes made by scientists have not *proved* that all animals with large brains are smart, or that all animals with small brains are stupid.

We do have another method that helps to tell us how smart an animal is. We can study how an animal *behaves*. If an animal lives a complex life, one that requires making many decisions, we can be fairly sure that it is a smart animal. Fossil evidence has given us an idea of how dinosaurs of the past and pterosaurs behaved. From what has been gathered, it does not appear that any were actually stupid.

We have already seen that the brain size of the coelurosaurs, dromaeosaurs, and the pterosaurs suggests that they were smart animals. Paleontologists believe that the behavior of these animals suggests the same thing, for it seems these animals made many decisions throughout their lives. They all hunted live prey and yet had to avoid dangerous predators. With their large eyes and long hands for grasping, coelurosaurs and dromaeosaurs were very swift predators of small game. No doubt they also scavenged. They lived by their cunning and their speed. Pterosaurs additionally had to keep their fur in good condition, plus they cared for their young. An animal that cares for its young needs to be good at recognizing danger. It must also be good at identifying its own offspring. These things require a good mind.

You may recall that the fossil record proves that sauropods traveled in herds. Paleontologists believe that ceratopsians (the four-legged "horned dinosaurs") traveled in herds too, because the fossils of them are often found bunched together in large numbers. Iguanodont (iguanodonts were large bipedal plant-eaters) fossils have also been found bunched together in large numbers, so they probably went in herds as well. Traveling in a herd usually requires mental skills. The animals that do so must be able to communicate with one another. We can therefore assume that these dinosaurs had a good amount of mental development.

Finally, there is fossil evidence (known as the Davenport Ranch site) of sauropod footprints where small ones are in the center of a trail and large prints are along the outer edge. Were large adults protecting

Although short-crested, *Triceratops* was the largest of the ceratopsians, reaching 30 feet (9 m) in length and weighing 8 tons.

their young as they moved along? It seems so. This certainly is not something that stupid animals do.

In conclusion, we may say that all evidence indicates that the pterosaurs and the coelurosaurs and dromaeosaurs all were fairly smart animals. (Of course we can use our knowledge of birds to support our conclusion about coelurosaurs. Despite the unflattering phrase "birdbrain," we know that birds are quite smart.)

As for the huge dinosaurs, things are not so clear. The brain size of the giants suggests that they were not particularly smart animals. But from what we are learning about their behavior, we cannot say they were stupid. Perhaps the wisest thing we can do is hold our judgement until we learn more.

Unfortunately, many people still believe that the dinosaurs were stupid and that they became extinct because of it. This is nonsense. The survival of a species is not based on skill or strength or smartness. It is based on how well-suited the species is to its environment. Because all pterosaurs and all dinosaurs except the line of coelurosaurs, which became our modern birds, became extinct, something must have happened to make them unsuitable. Let's turn now to this problem.

70 Million Years Ago: Devastation

The end of the age of the dinosaurs came at the close of the Cretaceous period, almost 70 million years ago. Except for birds, no trace of the dinosaurs can be found from a time period after that. Dinosaurs, however, were not the only animals that died out then. The pterosaurs also did. In the seas, the plesiosaurs (large marine reptiles) and mosasaurs (large marine lizards) died out, and so did the ammonites (tentacled molluscs that lived in chambered shells) and chalk-forming plankton (free-floating microscopic animals that lived in shells). Many kinds of plants also died out.

These life forms altogether made up a great part of all the living things on Earth at that time. As to the life forms that did not die out, such as the mammals, something also happened: There were suddenly less of them! Thus, at the close of the Cretaceous period the earth became lonely and barren compared to the earlier times. Something had robbed the earth of most of its inhabitants. Something had *devastated* it. The extinction of the great dinosaurs was part of this devastation. Therefore, if we want to find out why dinosaurs became extinct, we should not be looking for an explanation that tells about just them only. We must try to find an explanation that fits *all* the extinct life forms of that time period. The correct explanation should also tell about the surviving life forms: it should explain why their numbers were reduced, and it should explain why they survived at all.

Different explanations have been offered by scientists. However, before we discuss them, we must know a bit about the survivors. This will enable us to find the most convincing explanation.

The life forms that survived were the *smallest* or *least numerous* of all the living things of the Cretaceous period. For example, conifers ("evergreens") survived to replace the cycads (palmlike trees), which had earlier been abundant.

Among animals, the iguanas, tuataras, monitor lizards and the smaller crocodiles survived. The smaller turtles and the few snakes did too. The mammals also

Much of the life in the seas suffered extinction at the end of the Mesozoic era. The long-tailed animal pictured to the left is *Tylosaurus*, one of the best known mosasaurs, which were large marine lizards similar in some ways to today's monitor lizards. *Tylosaurus* fed on ammonites and reached a length of 26 feet (7.8 m). Some mosasaurs, however, grew to twice this length.

In the upper right is a long-necked plesiosaur, *Elasmosaurus*. Long-necked plesiosaurs were marine or freshwater reptiles that had limb structure suitable for fast, agile swimming. They were probably surface-dwellers that fed on fish. *Elasmosaurus* had the longest neck of all known plesiosaurs. From head to tail *Elasmosaurus* measured 33 feet (10 m).

Bottom right is *Peloneustes*, a short-necked plesiosaur. The short-necked plesiosaurs were built for powerful, long-distance swimming. They fed on cephalopods. *Peloneustes* grew to be 8 feet (2.4 m) long, while other short-necked plesiosaurs were as much as 40 feet (12 m) in length.

In the circle is an ammonite, a marine mollusc (cephalopod) very similar to today's chambered nautilus. Some fossilized ammonite shells have been found having a diameter of more than 8 feet (2.4 m). Ammonites seem to have been surface dwellers.

---

survived, of course, and they were remarkably tiny. (A typical early mammal such as *Megazostrodon* was small enough to have nestled in the palm of your hand. Later mammals were often larger, but not by much. The biggest were not much larger than a house cat, and one such animal—the Virginia Opossum—is still with us, easily seen throughout much of North America.) Despite a sudden reduction in their populations, all these groups of animals continued to survive right to the present time. The mammals, as we know, eventually increased their numbers and their size. We might say that they are the dominant land animal today (if we do not count the insects).

We are now ready to examine various explanations that have been offered to tell why dinosaurs died out. Each explanation is actually something that a scientist or group of scientists *assumes* or *imagines* is true. It is not something meant to be accepted as absolute truth, unquestioned. In fact, it is created to encourage questions. We call this type of explanation a *hypothesis*. Hypotheses (the plural of hypothesis) are meant to be tested, to see how convincing they are. One that is very convincing is likely to be correct and is therefore accepted as true—with some reservation: There is always the possibility new evidence will be found to destroy the believability of an accepted hypothesis. So scientists reserve their right to reject any one of them, no matter how convincing it may appear to be. Nevertheless, a number of hypotheses throughout our history have come to be accepted as scientific fact. The "heliocentric theory of the solar system,"

Megazostrodon was one of the very earliest mammals inhabiting our earth about 195 million years ago. It was only 4 inches (10 cm) long and resembled today's shrew.

which says the sun is in the center of our solar system, is an example. It was once just another hypothesis.

Through the years, many different hypotheses have been offered to explain what happened to the dinosaurs. We shall take the more popular ones and test them against the new information scientists have gathered, to try to find the one that is most convincing.

Hypothesis: Mammals caused the extinctions by eating dinosaur eggs. This is among the least convincing of all the hypotheses. In the first place, we know that the mammal population suffered a loss in numbers. If they were eating greater amounts of dinosaur eggs, we would expect that there would have been more of them, not less.

Secondly, mammals came into existence around 200 million years ago. This means that for the *one hundred and thirty million years* before the extinction of dinosaurs mammals had no bad effects on them. No reason is given why they should have suddenly wiped out the dinosaurs after all that time.

A third point that makes this hypothesis unconvincing is that it cannot explain why the pterosaurs died out, or why much of the marine life died out, or why some of the plant life died out. There is also the problem of the dinosaurs that some scientists believe did not lay eggs. Why did they become extinct?

Finally, it does not tell why mammals did not cause the extinction of crocodiles, lizards, or snakes by eating *their* eggs. In other words, this hypothesis expects us to believe that mammals ate very few, if any, reptile eggs. But it doesn't say why. This hypothesis, therefore, is no longer accepted by most scientists.

Hypothesis: Dinosaurs became extinct because they became senile. This hypothesis explains that entire species age and, like some very old persons, become senile and weak, eventually dying under the pressures of their environment. This may seem silly to us now, but it was seriously considered as recently as the 1950s. It is an unconvincing hypothesis because it cannot explain why the mosasaurs in the seas died out. For mosasaurs had only made their appearance during the middle of the Cretaceous period, so they were surely not a very "old" species when they died out.

The hypothesis also cannot explain why so many "old" species such as the crocodiles and tuataras did *not* die out.

Today, almost no one accepts this hypothesis.

Hypothesis: Poisonous plants killed off the dinosaurs. This hypothesis goes like this: Almost 125 million years ago flowering plants came about. These plants contained highly poisonous alkaloids, which are bitter or salty-tasting substances. We know that turtles cannot detect these poisons as well as mammals can, so they eat them until it is too late. By the time they sense the bad-tasting poisons, they have already eaten enough to kill themselves. The plant-eating dinosaurs probably were the same way—since they were reptiles like turtles—and they died out because of it. The meat-eating dinosaurs died out because they lost their food source, the plant-eating dinosaurs. Mammals survived because they did not eat the bad-tasting poisonous plants. After all, they were able to sense the bad-tasting plants right away.

At first glance this hypothesis may seem convincing. But there are many things wrong with it. First, it assumes that the plant-eating dinosaurs were reptiles like turtles! We know that this was not the case. Dinosaurs of the past, like the birds of today, differed from turtles as much as mammals do. Therefore, there is absolutely no reason to think that any dinosaur would have eaten poisonous plants as a turtle does.

A second problem has to do with the appearance of the flowering plants. They appeared almost 125 million years ago. So the dinosaurs had been living their lives for *fifty-five million years* while flowering plants were developing and growing without being poisoned by them. The hypothesis does not explain how this could have happened.

A third problem is the fact that many plant-eating dinosaurs did not live off flowering plants. For example, the "duck-billed" hadrosaurs, with their special grinding teeth, ate very tough, abrasive plants, not soft, flowering plants. Why they perished is not explained.

There are also the problems of the marine life and

The plant-eating ceratopsians were of two types: long-crested, and short-crested. *Chasmosaurus* (also named *Protosaurus*) was a long-crested type, reaching 26 feet (7.8 m) in length and weighing perhaps 5 tons.

the pterosaurs. This hypothesis cannot explain their extinction.

With so many problems, this hypothesis is not convincing.

Hypothesis: A cosmic explosion devastated the Earth. This is a very interesting hypothesis, for it does take into account all the living things on earth at the close of the Cretaceous period. It attempts to tell why some became extinct and why some did not.

The hypothesis explains that every so often a massive exploding star, called a *supernova,* occurs in our galaxy or in one nearby. Each one showers the earth with radioactive particles. However, most supernovae are so far away that the radiation levels are very low. But closer ones do occur every few hundred million years or so. This means that there could have been one that occurred at the Cretaceous period's end. A nearby supernova would have bombarded Earth with a level of ultraviolet radiation deadly to many life forms. The dinosaurs, being so large and unprotected, would have quickly perished. The pterosaurs, soaring in the open skies, also would have received massive deadly amounts of the radiation. In the seas, the plesiosaurs and mosasaurs might have easily perished from radiation poisoning.

The chalk-forming plankton, however, are a different story. They were simple life forms, and simple life forms are actually quite tough in resisting the harm from ultraviolet radiation. We know that those of today require about *ten times* as much radiation as most mammals do to be killed. Plankton of 70 million years ago must have been just as tough. In addition, the chalk-forming plankton lived in water, which would have given them a certain amount of protection. Therefore, in order for them to have been killed by radiation, the level of it would have had to have been massive. Yet a massive level of harmful radiation would certainly have killed all of the mammals. Obviously this did not happen. So here is a serious problem for the hypothesis.

Some scientists claim there is another problem with the hypothesis. They agree that the end of the great dinosaurs came abruptly. It may have taken just a million years (a span of a million years is a blink of an eye in geologic time, for the earth is 4.6 *billion* years old); or possibly it took much less time, only hundreds of years. But the fossil record shows that it was a *progressive* event, no matter how short a time it took. By this it is meant that once the various dinosaurs began dying out, the rate of the deaths speeded up until there were no great dinosaurs at all. The marine fossil record shows the same thing. Therefore, the dying off of the species started slowly and built up speed until the end. This is opposite what we would expect to occur from a massive shower of deadly radiation. In such a case, the number of deaths would almost certainly be very high right at the beginning, and then would dwindle until the end.

The "supernova hypothesis" is far from completely convincing, but it may not be entirely wrong. For it may tie in with the most convincing hypothesis of all. This hypothesis deals with *climate.*

Hypothesis: A severe cold spell caused the extinctions. The final hypothesis we shall discuss says that an extreme cold spell swept the entire earth at the close of the Cretaceous period. This cold spell, we are told, caused the extinction of the various life forms that died out and the reduction in the numbers of those life forms that survived.

Because our primary concern is with the dinosaurs, we'll take them first. The "cold climate" hypothesis offers a simple explanation of why cold climate killed off the great dinosaurs: They had no insulation to protect themselves from it. You may recall that all dinosaurs except the smallest coelurosaurs had become large to keep their body warmth. Instead of in-

Scolosaurus was a heavily built ankylosaur, weighing 3 to 5 tons despite its having been only 13 feet (3.9 m) long.

sulation, they had great size. In that form they were able to withstand cool temperatures. But they were not designed to withstand *extreme* cold. Any large animal with no insulation suffers in days and days of terribly cold weather. *Years* of it would mean certain death for the entire species.

What effect did the cold have on the species of animals that survived? We have evidence to indicate that many of the individual animals from the surviving species did not live. The hypothesis says that it was the sudden cold climate that killed off many right away, thereby reducing the numbers of the individuals in all the surviving species.

Of course, some individuals did survive to produce offspring. The *mammals* were probably best off, for they had fur as insulation, and they could have easily burrowed to keep warm. *Birds* also had insulation, in the form of feathers. Nesting also probably helped their survival. We must emphasize that the birds represent the coelurosaurian line of dinosaurs. It makes good sense that they were the only dinosaurs to have survived: They were the only ones with insulation to protect themselves from extreme cold.

Reptiles in cold temperatures become sluggish and cold. But they often can survive because they can burrow and hibernate. The great dinosaurs were not suited for hibernation. They were too large to do it safely; and for a "warm-blooded" animal to hibernate it should have insulation.

The "cold climate hypothesis" seems convincing so far. How does it hold up when we consider the *marine life* and the *land plants*?

The animals of the sea that perished at the Cretaceous period's end had lived in the *surface waters*. These waters were relatively shallow and were heated by the sun. The life forms that lived there were accustomed to warm temperatures. Cold climate would have had a great effect on the temperature of these waters. If it became extremely cold, we would expect many life forms there to have perished. The fossil record shows that indeed many *did* perish. Plesiosaurs, mosasaurs, ammonites, and the chalk-forming plankton all died out.

Additionally, we may consider the deeper waters. They are cold, and air temperature has little effect there. The marine life forms residing there are accustomed to the cold temperatures. They probably would spread to any warm waters that turned cold. The fossil record indicates that cold-water life *did increase* around 70 million years ago. This strongly suggests that the waters overall did turn colder.

Therefore, the marine life extinctions fit well into the "cold climate hypothesis"; and the increase of the cold-water life does too.

In general, the land plants changed from tropical types to types that did better in the colder, temperate climates. Evergreen conifers, for example, replaced the cycads. (Cycads today live only in warm, stable climates. They are similar to palm trees.) Even the flowering plants, which had recently become abundant, were almost completely replaced by the conifers. So, the plants also support the hypothesis: It appears that they became surrounded by cold climate.

Can the cold climate hypothesis explain why the *pterosaurs* became extinct? They were insulated by their fur. If birds survived, we might expect that pterosaurs would have survived too. But let us think a moment. Pterosaurs differed from birds in the manner in which they flew. Birds that fly flap their wings; those that shared the sky with the pterosaurs did so too. But the pterosaurs *glided*. They were masters of gliding, capable of becoming airborne on a breeze less than 15 miles (24 km) per hour. And remember, their skeletons were extremely delicate; they made birds seem thick by comparison. Thin, delicate bones were a great advantage for soaring in gentle breezes, but they could never be an advantage in *strong winds*. Scientists believe that strong winds did indeed come with the cold spell. In particular, the winds called Westerlies and Trade Winds became strong. This happened, we are told, because the temperature at the Earth's poles and the temperature at the Earth's equator became very different from each other, much more different than before. Scientists guess that winds came that were well above 30 miles (48 km) per hour. Such winds were fatal to the pterosaurs. You see, pterosaurs were so perfectly adapted to the gentle wind conditions of their skies that any change that brought winds above 25 miles (40 km) per hour would have made it impossible for them to glide. Neither their "swing-back" wings nor their "parachute" membranes would have enabled the pterosaurs to maneuver through winds that strong. Therefore, cold climate that brought with it severe winds spelled disaster for the pterosaurs.

The cold climate hypothesis is very impressive. It appears to be correct. It takes into account both the victims and the survivors. It also agrees with what we know about *biological advantages:* They could easily become disadvantages.

The extinctions of the great dinosaurs and pterosaurs are examples of this. Through evolution, all of the dinosaurs except coelurosaurs became very large. This was their biological advantage—large size itself. It enabled the dinosaurs to dominate their world; it was their specialty.

Pterosaurs also had a specialty. Although they certainly were huge, their real specialty was gliding. (Because of superior muscles, the birds had replaced the small pterosaurs by beating them to their prey, the insects. This "forced" the pterosaurs to specialize in gliding.)

Great size was a biological advantage for dinosaurs, and a great ability to glide was a biological advantage for pterosaurs. Each advantage brought tremendous success. But the sudden climatic change turned the advantages, which had worked so well for millions and millions of years, into disadvantages. Both the large dinosaurs and pterosaurs were trapped. The large dinosaurs needed insulation, but they had

The ankylosaur *Euplocephalus* (also named *Ankylosaurus,* and *Stereocephalus*) was 15 to 16.5 feet (4.5–4.9 m) long and weighed 3 to 5 tons.

specialized in doing without it. Pterosaurs needed the skeleton and muscles that would have been good for flapping their wings, but they had specialized in doing without them. There was no going back. They were doomed.

What caused the extreme cold that swept the earth? Scientists simply do not know for sure what caused it. Apparently it did not come in the same way that an "ice age" comes; and it did not last long enough to cause any glaciers to form. Some scientists believe that it was a *supernova* that caused it.

Radiation from a fairly near supernova would destroy the ability of the earth's atmosphere to hold warmth. It would also cause a blanket of ice to form above the atmosphere that would shield the earth from the sun's warming rays. Something like this may have happened at the end of the Cretaceous period. So it is possible that a supernova too far away to poison the earth with deadly radiation did harm its life forms anyway, by causing freezing temperatures.

Other scientists believe the cold spell came from a *drop in the sea level*. According to these scientists, a drop in the sea level occurred because the earth's crust under the seas sunk. The seas moved away from the edges of the continents to fill the space left by the sunken earth.

It is true that a drop in the sea level great enough to cause the seas to move away from the edge (shelf, actually) of each continent would cause a cold spell to occur. But we can't be certain such a thing did happen almost 70 million years ago.

Another possibility is an asteroid collision. There is evidence that a very large asteroid may have collided with the earth about 70 million years ago. Dustlike pulverized rock, resulting from the impact of the collision, would have spread all throughout the earth's atmosphere. This would have blocked off the warming rays of the sun.

Whatever caused it, the cold spell changed the forms of life that inhabit Earth. In one brief moment in geologic time, it ended the long history of the largest animals to have ever walked the land and soared the sky.

The Importance of Dinosaurs

Actually, all life forms are the same age. The history of each one can be traced back almost 3.8 billion years to the first signs of life. When we call a species "old" or "young" we do it only to give the species a place in the whole history of life on earth. It is not done to make us think that life forms are separate from each other. All life may be thought of as one great long chain, extending from the distant past to the present.

Each "link" in our chain is just as important as the next one. But scientists do like to pinpoint when each major movement or change occurred in the history of life. *Upright leg posture* is considered to be a major change that happened to animals sometime in the Mesozoic era. Scientists would like to know exactly when

126

MILLIONS   ERA
OF YEARS
AGO | CENOZOIC | First mammals
     | MESOZOIC |
     | PALEOZOIC |
500 | | First dinosaurs
     | | First reptiles
     | | First land plants
1,000 | PRECAMBRIAN | First fish
     | | First
     | | pterosaurs

1,500 | First complex life forms
       leading to animal life

2,000

2,500   Although the dinosaurs
               dominated the land for
               over 140 million years,
               their time represents a
3,000   small portion of Earth's
               history.

3,500

       First signs of life

4,000

4,500 Hardening of earth's crust

it evolved, and which animals first had it. Until recently, mammals were given credit for being the first animals to travel with their legs upright, inserted under their bodies. We know now we made a mistake here. For dinosaurs also traveled with their legs upright, and this makes them important.

There is also *bipedalism.* Scientists who study the biological history of human beings often mention our bipedal posture. They believe it played an important part in our becoming smart animals. If we agree that it did, we must give more respect to the dinosaurs. Many of them traveled upright on two legs. In fact, their direct ancestors, the pseudosuchian thecodonts, were the *first* animals to have done so. The dinosaurs *mastered* it, and did so even though they were heavy in bodyweight.

We must also say dinosaurs are important in the history of life because they are still with us: Imagine our world without birds! They certainly are a great part of the earth's living system.

Yet another reason for the importance of dinosaurs can be found in the history of the science known as *natural history.* Until the discovery of dinosaur fossils, most people studying natural history (the history of things in nature) did not believe in evolution and its "laws." The fossils, however, helped prove that species do evolve, and that they often become extinct.

The fact that so many dinosaurs and the pterosaurs did become extinct is also important—very important —for it shows us how delicate the balance of nature is. Who would have guessed that such large and varied animals, after dominating the land and sky for almost 140 million years, would suddenly perish? Perhaps this may affect our behavior and how we think of ourselves. People usually act as though the earth's living things and its resources will never run out. We also act as though we will be around forever. The dinosaurs and the pterosaurs have shown us that neither may be true.

The lesson we can take from their extinction is this: We must try to preserve what we have. If we badly upset the delicate balance of nature by pollution, or war, or by using up important resources, we surely will follow the great dinosaurs and pterosaurs into extinction.

The Future Keeps Chipping Away at the Past

We certainly do not have the complete story of the dinosaurs and pterosaurs. You may have noticed that when we find an answer to a big question, our answer often brings up a new question. This should not upset us, however, because if we are able to ask new questions it means that we have learned the answers to old ones.

Unfortunately, we cannot be sure that *all* of our answers are correct. In the past we have made many errors guessing about fossils. The very first fossilized dinosaur bone discovered was mistakenly thought to be a bone of a gigantic man who lived long, long ago! (The bone was found in the 1670s. It was probably one belonging to *Megalosaurus*. We do not know where the

Iguanodon, a large ornithopod, may be the ancestor to the "duck-billed" hadrosaurs. Adult iguanodonts measured up to 33 feet (10 m) in length and weighed 4 to 7 tons.

bone is today.) There were also errors made the first time that a dinosaur was fully reconstructed. The large, spikelike thumb bone of *Iguanodon* was put on its nose, as a horn! In addition, *Iguanodon* was thought to have been quadrupedal (four-footed). In fact, all dinosaurs were thought to have been. A brilliant man named Joseph Leidy eventually realized that many were bipedal.

Another famous error in putting together a fossilized skeleton was made by the well-known paleontologist, Edward Drinker Cope. Professor Cope attached the head of a plesiosaur on the wrong end: He put it at the tip of the tail instead of the neck!

These kinds of errors happened because paleontology was a completely new science. The giant fossils were of animals that no one had known anything about. Scientists were forced to use their imagination to explain about them. Their hypotheses were often incorrect.

Today the science of paleontology is older. Paleontologists now have much more information to work with. Many fields of science offer help, and there are better methods of studying fossils. But we cannot be certain that the latest story of the dinosaurs and pterosaurs does not include errors. If there are errors, we will not know until new evidence tells us so. Most of this kind of evidence has yet to be uncovered. It may be in the form of a new fossil discovery, or it may be a new method of analyzing fossils.

New evidence is in the *future*, yet it will tell us about the *past*. This is what we mean when we say, "The future keeps chipping away at the past." This saying is especially suitable for paleontology: With each chip made by the chisel of the paleontologist, we learn more about life's past. We hope that in the future we do get answers to many of our unanswered questions, and that much of the incomplete story is filled in.

At this time the story of the great dinosaurs and

pterosaurs says that they were spectacular animals. Dinosaurs in particular have been very important in the long chain of life. Their story rests here—until the next discovery.

Glossary

Age of reptiles: This includes the four geologic periods, Permian, Triassic, Jurassic, and Cretaceous. It was believed that reptiles dominated throughout these periods. However, this is not a good phrase at all. *Dinosaurs* dominated the land for most of this time, and they were not reptiles. We may also mention the marine life: To the scientist studying life in the seas, this was the "age of the mollusc."

Ammonites: They were tentacled molluscs that lived in chambered shells, most of which were coiled. Ammonites were highly developed and were part of the cephalopod group, which includes the squid, octopus, cuttlefish, and nautilus. At the close of the Cretaceous period the ammonites became extinct.

Ankylosaurs: They were the "armored dinosaurs" that made up one of the four groups belonging in the *Ornithischia* order.

Archosaurs: They include thecodonts, dinosaurs, pterosaurs, birds, and crocodiles.

Aves: This is the class which birds are put into.

Bipedal: This word simply means "two-footed." Bipedal posture evolved about 220 million years ago in the dinosaur ancestor, the pseudosuchian thecodont. Many dinosaurs (all theropods and ornithopods) traveled bipedally, and the birds of today retain this trait.

Ceratopsians: They were the "horned dinosaurs" that made up one of the four groups belonging in the *Ornithischia* order.

Cycads: These plants were abundant during the Triassic and Jurassic periods. They were a bit like palm trees but had fernlike leaves. Most of them died at the end of the Cretaceous period, but some exist today in tropical regions.

Dinosaur: The name "dinosauria" was coined in 1841 by a British anatomy professor named Richard Owen. It was formed from two Greek words, *deinos*, meaning "terrible," and *saurus*, meaning "lizard." Today, some animals we call dinosaurs are scientifically called ornithischians, while others are saurischians. All dinosaurs except the coelurosaurs (birds) are extinct.

Ectothermic: This is the scientific term for "cold-blooded." A "cold-blooded" animal gets its insides warmed from outside temperatures. Its internal temperature varies.

Endothermic: This is the scientific term for "warm-blooded." A "warm-blooded" animal gets its insides warmed by its metabolic activities. Its internal temperature does not vary (although the hibernating "warm-blooded" animal's temperature is lowered during hibernation).

Evolution: Life has moved along in a certain way to change. We call this evolution. It is continual, gradual, and takes a long time.

Fossil: "Fossil" comes from the Latin word meaning "dug up." Any remains, impressions, or traces of life forms of the past that have been preserved we call fossils. Most of them are, in fact, dug up.

There are different kinds of fossils. Sometimes the form of the living thing itself has been preserved, encased in something hard. Other times it is petrified, meaning some of the chemicals that made up the form have changed through time, and the form has become stonelike.

Often we find a *cast* of a life form from the

past. A cast is made by the filling with sand or mud or chalk of a hollow space in the earth left by a life form after it has decayed. This happens when a dying or dead life form falls into sand or mud and becomes buried. With the passing of time the sand or mud hardens, encasing the life form. Soon the life form decays and crumbles, leaving a hollow space. Eventually this space is filled with soft sand or mud, and finally the "filling" becomes petrified. We end up with a cast, sometimes nearly perfect, of the life form. Usually it is only animals with hard skeletons that are fossilized in this manner.

Other fossils are called *trace fossils*. They include footprints, tracks, borings, and droppings of animals. Trace fossils may also be of nonliving things, such as the fossilized marks left by raindrops.

Gastrolith: This is a stone that an animal swallows. The stone does the job of teeth, but inside the stomach or gizzard, aiding digestion. Some ornithischians and sauropods used gastroliths. Today, some birds and some reptiles use them.

Geologic Time: Geologists are scientists who explain the history of the earth and its life forms by studying rocks. We have learned from them that our planet is about 4.6 billion years old. It has also been estimated that the first living things developed almost 3.8 billion years ago. To help make it easier to discuss such things of so long ago, scientists have divided the history of the earth into a geologic time scale. In each division different things happened: New mountains occurred, or old ones disintegrated; or new life forms developed, or old ones died out.

Ginkgoes: Ginkgoes were trees that grew almost everywhere during the dinosaur age. Some species grew to be more than 100 feet (30 m) tall. Today only one species, *Ginkgo biloba*, survives.

Metabolism: This includes all the activities that go on inside the body. It includes the breaking down and building up of cells and tissue, digestion of food, and it provides energy. A "warm-blooded" animal has a fast, or high, metabolism; a "cold-blooded" animal has a slow, or low, one.

Mosasaurs: They were large marine lizards that lived toward the end of the Cretaceous period. They seem to have been fierce predators. There are fossilized ammonite shells showing mosasaur teeth marks, so scientists assume ammonites made up at least part of the mosasaur's diet. At the close of the Cretaceous period, the mosasaurs became extinct.

Ornithischia: This is one of the two orders of dinosaurs. Ornithischians had birdlike pelvic bones, and almost all of them were plant-eaters. They include ornithopods, (iguanodonts, hadrosaurs, and pachycephalosaurs), stegosaurs, ankylosaurs, and ceratopsians. At the end of the dinosaur age, most dinosaurs were ornithischians. All of them suffered extinction at the Cretaceous period's end.

Ornithopods: They were the bipedal ornithischian dinosaurs, including iguanodonts, hadrosaurs, and pachycephalosaurs.

Paleontology: This is the science of studying life of the distant past that is recorded in the fossil record. Paleontologists, scientists who study fossils, must be good detectives, for most of the remains of life that they study are far from perfect.

Pangaea: Around 225 million years ago, all the continents we know today were joined together, forming one vast supercontinent, called Pangaea. In time, Pangaea split in two, forming *Laurasia* in the north, and *Gondwanaland* in the south. By the end of the Cretaceous period, the continents we have today had formed from these two splitting apart.

Plankton: They are tiny plants and animals that have little or no locomotion of their own in the seas. They float along in the water. The chalk-forming plankton, called *foraminifera*, are microscopic animals that live in shells. A particular type of them was abundant during most of the Mesozoic era, but became extinct at its end. Their shells have sunk to the sea bottoms or sea shelves and have turned to chalk. The famous White Cliffs of Dover were formed in this way.

Plesiosaurs: They were large marine or freshwater reptiles that lived throughout the Mesozoic era. There were two kinds: long-necked, and short-necked. They all became extinct at the end of the Cretaceous period.

Pseudosuchians: They were one type of the thecodonts of the Triassic period. They were the first animals to travel bipedally, and they were ancestors to the dinosaurs and pterosaurs.

Quadrupedal: This word means "four-footed." Among the saurischian dinosaurs it was the sauropods that traveled quadrupedally (on four feet); among the ornithischian dinosaurs, it was the stegosaurs, ankylosaurs, and ceratopsians.

Saurischia: This is one of the two orders of dinosaurs. Scientists of the 1800s believed that the saurischian pelvis was lizardlike, and this was the basis for forming the saurischian order. It includes the sauropods and theropods. At the beginning of the dinosaur age, most dinosaurs were saurischians. Some are still with us: The coelurosaurs, part of the theropod group, survived because they evolved into feathered dinosaurs (birds).

Sauropods: They were the huge quadrupedal saurischian dinosaurs. They had long necks and tails, and were plant-eaters.

Stegosaurs: They were one of the four groups belonging in the *Ornithischia* order. They had bony plates along the ridge of their spine. They were apparently replaced early in the Cretaceous period by the ankylosaurs.

Supernova: A large star that ends its existence by a spectacular explosion is called a supernova. The light that comes from a supernova is brighter than the entire galaxy it belongs to. Some scientists believe that a nearby supernova ended the "reign" of the dinosaurs, either by direct, harmful radiation, or by causing the great cold spell that swept the earth almost 70 million years ago.

Taxonomy: This is the science of classifying life forms.

Thecodonts: They were reptilelike animals of the Triassic period. They were the aetosaurs, phytosaurs, and the ancestors to the dinosaurs, the pseudosuchians.

Therapsids: They were animals of the late Permian period and early Triassic period. They had characteristics of both reptiles *and* mammals. For thirty million years they were the dominant land animals, but eventually they gave way to the thecodonts. Therapsids are ancestors to the mammals.

Theropods: They were the bipedal, flesh-eating dinosaurs in the *Saurischia* order. They include carnosaurs, coelurosaurs and dromaeosaurs.

Index

Page numbers in bold face indicate illustrations

T

W

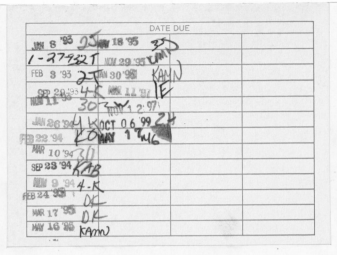

DATE DUE		
JAN 8 '93 25	NOV 18 '95 35	
1-27-93 2T	NOV 29 '95 UMN	
FEB 3 '93 2T	JAN 30 '96 KAMN	
SEP 20 '93 4K	MAR 11 '97 IE	
NOV 11 '93 30	NOV 12 '97	
JAN 26 '94 4 K	OCT 06 '99 2K	
FEB 22 '94 KO	MAY 17 '06 MG	
MAR 10 '94 BU		
SEP 23 '94 KAB		
NOV 9 '94 4-K		
FEB 24 '95 OK		
MAR 17 '95 DK		
MAY 16 '95 KAMN		

567.9
MAN

Mannetti, William.

Dinosaurs in your
back yard.

12176

$11.01

PETOSKEY ELEMENTARY LIBRARIES